W9-ACU-500

Ride to Vengeance

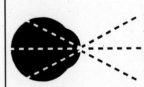

This Large Print Book carries the
Seal of Approval of N.A.V.H.

A RIDGE PARKMAN WESTERN

RIDE TO VENGEANCE

GREG HUNT

THORNDIKE PRESS

A part of Gale, Cengage Learning

GALE
CENGAGE Learning·

Farmington Hills, Mich • San Francisco • New York • Waterville, Maine
Meriden, Conn • Mason, Ohio • Chicago

GALE
CENGAGE Learning®

LIBRARY OF CONGRESS CATALOGING-IN-PUBLICATION DATA

Names: Hunt, Greg, 1947– author.
Title: Ride to vengeance : a Ridge Parkman western / by Greg Hunt.
Description: Large print edition. | Waterville, Maine : Thorndike Press, 2016. |
  Series: Thorndike Press large print western
Identifiers: LCCN 2016010619| ISBN 9781410489685 (hardcover) | ISBN 141048968X
  (hardcover)
Subjects: LCSH: Large type books. | GSAFD: Western stories.
Classification: LCC PS3558.U46768 R53 2016 | DDC 813/.54—dc23
LC record available at https://lccn.loc.gov/2016010619

Published in 2016 by arrangement with Greg Hunt

Printed in Mexico
1 2 3 4 5 6 7 20 19 18 17 16

Ride to Vengeance

CHAPTER ONE

The wagon driver seemed oblivious to the thudding of the cannons and the increasing crack of rifle fire ahead. His whole concentration was aimed at keeping the horses going at top speed and keeping the wagon on the road. He knew a battle was probably beginning up ahead and that at any moment a stray bullet might find his cargo of cannon powder and shot and end it all for him, but in two years of driving such loads into the midst of dozens of battles and skirmishes, he had learned to pay attention only to his driving and to let the possibilities be damned.

The five men in the back of the wagon, however, felt differently. Four of them saw in the advancing line of blue uniforms on the distant hill a chance for freedom after many months of captivity.

The fifth, distinguishable from the others by his gray tunic and hat and his shotgun, saw in the situation the real possibility that he could die. One of the four prisoners, heartened by the nearness of freedom, might jump him, or a Union bullet might reach the powder in the wagon with them, or a Union bullet might reach him. He braced himself and watched his prisoners tensely, unwilling to admit his fear even to himself.

One of the four prisoners, Ben Halpert, considered the scene with mixed emotions. A year ago, at twenty, he would have viewed those distant soldiers as the enemy because then he had been a Confederate soldier and a patriot of the South. But since that time he had been made a prisoner of his own country for refusing to take an order, and his political views and loyalties had faded and finally disappeared in the more immediate struggle to stay alive.

He no longer saw any reason to be loyal to a government which let such men as Major Lester Salem, the prison commander, use the excuse of war to steal and murder for his own gain. A year before, Ben had been able to nobly hate an enemy for the sake of his country, but since then he had learned to hate in a much more personal and less noble way. He had learned to hate a guard who had clubbed him until he could not walk because he had talked back, or a fellow prisoner who stole his food. And he had learned to hate the man who had put him there with a deep abiding hatred, which he knew would continue to burn inside him until one of them was dead.

As Ben watched the Union soldiers running and shooting and being shot and continuing their charge down the hill, he wondered, if he fell into their hands, whether they would put him into another prison camp because he had been a Confederate soldier or free him because he was a Confederate prisoner. He also watched the guard in the wagon with him, wondering whether he could take this big man with only his bare hands. Janson, despite his size, was quick and alert, and Ben knew that he was ruthlessly suited to his work. If Ben attacked and failed, the punishment that followed would be brutal. He finally decided to wait and take his chances after they arrived at the battlefront. If they became a part of the rout that appeared to be shaping up, he would surely have at least one chance to escape, and one chance was all he needed.

Nearer the battle the driver turned off the main road and started up the hill opposite the Union positions. The Confederate cannons were located on this hill. As they rose, the scene below was more easily seen. The Confederate troops below were being steadily pushed back toward a small wood. They might have been able to make a stand there, but in some places there were just no men to resist the blue tide, so it seemed that they would eventually be flanked and surrounded.

The cannons above continued to blast, but Ben could see that the explosions below were as often among their own side as among the enemy. There was obviously no battle plan for the Confederate side, and leadership and organization were rapidly deteriorating.

Despite his own situation, Ben hated to see it end this way. There was no nobility in this defeat, no shred of pride or valor that the few survivors could hold onto so that it would seem to have some purpose and reason. It was just slaughter. Men were dying senselessly here in a vain effort to hold ground that was not worth the shedding of one drop of blood. Men were dying because they wore the wrong color of clothes.

The wagon reached the top of the hill and they began to unload its contents in piles behind the cannons. Two officers joined Janson, and the three of them supervised the prisoners' work with clubs. Before they had finished, two more wagons arrived, and they spent the next hour trying to get the material to the cannons as fast as it could be fired.

The battle below disappeared into the woods, but as time passed, no soldiers from either army emerged from the other side. The attack had been successful, and it made sense that no Union commander would want to push his men up the hill directly into the cannon fire since the big guns would have to be pulled back tonight anyway. The Union army would probably be able to march forward all the next day with little opposition.

The cannons got the range of the woods and began pouring all their rounds into the middle of it, but before long Union cannons appeared on the opposite hill. Ben watched as the blasts from those cannons crept up the hill and got their range on the Confederate positions. He knew his chance would come soon in the midst of this artillery duel if he was not killed first. He decided which way he would run when the time came and he was unguarded for a moment.

Then the whole world seemed to blow up in his face.

It was a direct hit on a stack of powder kegs that they had just walked away from. Ben was blown several feet and was so stunned that he could not move for a moment. Finally he rose up onto one elbow and saw Janson on his hands and knees about ten feet away shaking his head like a groggy bull. One of the officers lay motionless and bloody beside him, and the other was nowhere in sight.

Finding that he could rise without too much pain, Ben got to his feet and staggered toward Janson. Using a wagon wheel spoke, he hit the guard so hard across the head that he threw himself off balance and fell across the body. Lying there with Janson's blood soaking through his shirt, Ben felt none of the deep, savage pleasure he had imagined he would feel. He felt hollow and alone, and he knew that he had broken the last link with that young, untried farm boy he had been not too long ago.

The changes in him had started two years before when a platoon of Confederate soldiers came and took him and several other boys his age away for military training. Throughout the next few months he had seen and done things that had made him less of a boy and more of a man. Life on the front lines was hard during that, the third year of the war, as victories for the South became more rare and defeats more disastrous.

Then Ben thought he had been given a break. He was made a guard in a prison camp far from the front. But during the first week of duty he made a moral decision, which affected the rest of his life. He refused to shoot a prisoner who tried to attack the camp commander, Major Salem. Ben knocked the man out, but when the major told him to shoot, he refused.

For that he was thrown in with the prisoners without a trial, and since that time he had been singled out repeatedly for special punishment and extra work.

The hatred that Ben had nurtured for Salem had gone a long way toward blotting out the last remaining semblances of youth that remained in him. Then one day a guard who had been a friend of Ben's told him that his home had been raided and burned by a band of renegades and that his father was dead. A wave of utter despair engulfed Ben for weeks after that, but when he did finally start recovering from the depths of grief, he emerged a different man, hard, merciless, and utterly unswerving in his desire for revenge. His father had been the last of his family, and there was nothing more for Ben to go home to ever. He was a man without a past.

Now, lying across the body of a man he had hated, he knew that his life had no direction except to survive and to kill Salem. In the smoke of the cannon fire and the explosions, no one had seen what he had done, or else no one cared. He rose and started away. All the previous plans of escape were forgotten. He just walked away from the battle.

CHAPTER TWO

The small stream wound its way raggedly between two steep-sided hills, circling rugged outcroppings of rock along the hillside and finally spilling into a small, clear pool at the base of the hills. One side of the pool faced an open, shell-pocked meadow, but the other bank was lined with trees and thick underbrush.

In his dazed escape of the day before, Ben had instinctively sought the shelter of the undergrowth. He woke in the morning stiff, bruised, and still bone weary, but he was accustomed to carrying on, to moving and working under these circumstances. The prison camp had given him that much. He crawled through the brush to the edge of the pool and drank greedily, then raised his eyes and surveyed his surroundings.

He had not heard the cannons stop firing during the night, but they now stood abandoned on the hill above him. Evidently the defeated rebel army had been forced to retreat so quickly that they had to leave behind even their priceless artillery. There was not a sign of life anywhere, but the signs of death were everywhere, witnessing that a big part of an army had been slaughtered from behind as it tried desperately to pull back.

He wondered if this was the way it was on the other fronts of the war. If the Union forces were as strong and efficient in other places as they had been here, he did not see how any of the Confederate leaders could hope to prolong the war more than a few more weeks.

That was what Ben wanted, for the war to end. When it was over he could begin his search for the man he knew must die before his own life could continue. He could only plan his future to the point when he would be standing over Major Salem's body, and the only goal of the plans that he began formulating was to prepare him for that moment.

Right then he knew one of the most urgent matters was to avoid falling into the hands of either army. He needed time to get rid of his identity as a Confederate criminal and to establish a new one. He needed time to become strong again and to plan.

He spent that day in the clump of trees, soaking in the pool to relieve the pain and stiffness that the explosion had caused and hiding when he heard horses or men in the area. Although it had been almost two days since he had eaten, he did not move from the cover of the trees until dark.

Chapter Three

Mac Firston sat by the fire, pitching an occasional twig into the flames and trying to figure out what to do next. He had always been good at making the right decisions when things were happening fast, but things had never before happened quite as fast as they had in the last couple of days.

It seemed easy enough when he and his men started out. They were just going to sweep in on a Union arms shipment, take as much as they could carry, and get out.

But word must have gotten out about the raid because the Yankees were waiting for them. Only half of the forty men who had ridden with him to attack the line of wagons rode away, and they had not taken a single rifle or round of ammunition. Then, as they were retreating headlong toward safety behind the Confederate lines, they ran into an ambush that had been set up and was waiting for them at exactly the right place.

When they finally reached their camp, scarcely a man of the twelve remaining did not have some sort of wound to show for the night's work. Firston himself had a flesh wound in the leg, which had bled considerably during the long ride back and made it hard for him to stay in the saddle.

They spent the next day patching their wounds and hoping that the battle that was going on nearby would not move in their direction. During the next night, after the cannon fire stopped, Firston had sent a scout out to see what was happening. He had returned only a few minutes before with the news that the Confederates had retreated to new positions five miles south and that the Union army, in its hasty pursuit, had swept right on by Firston's camp.

Now Firston found himself facing the decision of whether to lead what men could travel and to try to get back behind the retreating Southern forces or to just strike out and try to avoid capture until they were clear of the immediate battle area. Neither idea had any obvious merit except that both would get them away from this camp, which might be discovered and attacked by a Yankee patrol at any time.

If they went south there was no guarantee that they would get through, and if they did get through he was not at all sure he could find Major Salem, under whose protection his band had always operated.

It had been a nice setup for a while, though. Firston had put together a small band of renegades and, supplied with arms and ammunition from Salem, had made a business of raiding and looting small settlements in a hundred-mile radius of the area. Salem had taken a cut of the profits and had created for them the cover of a band of guerrillas operating against the Union. But without Salem that cover was weak because, besides the few times when he and his men had to fight when they met patrols, they had done little to advance the Southern cause.

Firston tried to think what Salem would probably do now that the prison camp was in Union hands. Any other officer would probably be reassigned to another unit that needed an officer of that rank. But leading a fighting unit in a desperate struggle to hold ground was probably not the kind of job Salem would undertake. Firston had never seen Salem show much loyalty to the Confederates, so now that the cause was going badly, he figured Salem had probably sought a quick means of escape.

After considering all that, Firston knew the only logical thing to do was to take the most direct route away from both armies. He had heard that there were places to the west where the war was only something a man read about in the papers and where lawmen were scarce. He had enough money to last his band until they got there, and they would find ways to get more once they were safe again.

Pleased that he finally had a direction figured out and had things to do, he rose and began walking among his men, seeing which ones would be able to ride and which would have to be left behind. They would have to move fast for the first few days, and he did not want anybody along who was likely to fall behind or who would need care. The ones who were left behind would have to take care of themselves. They had known what they were getting into when they decided to ride with him, and now they would just have to make the best of things on their own.

As Firston was saddling up, one of the men who was posted as guard came up to him. "We've caught a man tryin' to sneak into camp, Mac," he said. "Says he was just tryin' to get some food."

"Well, shoot him," Firston said impatiently. "We have to ride."

"He says he has some information which

will interest you."

Firston turned, anxious to get moving but knowing that any piece of information might be useful in getting out of danger. "Bring him here, then, but keep a gun on him."

The guard led a stranger up. His hands were tied, and there was a fresh cut on his cheek that was trickling blood down his face. Firston could see by the uniform that the man was one of the prisoners from Salem's camp.

He was young, but the traces of hard work and hard living were unmistakable in his face and in his bitter expression. Firston could see this man was tough enough to take the hard life of the prison camp, and probably more, without having his spirit broken, and smart enough that he could be a real threat to anyone he did not like. He was shuffling now, either from hunger or exhaustion or both, and he looked as if he had been on a quick trip through hell in the last few days.

"Whatever you know is goin' to have to be damn good to buy your life," Firston said. "What's your name an' what were you doin' sneakin' into my camp?"

"The name's Ben Halpert," the prisoner answered. "I thought I might be able to get some food here. I didn't know whose camp it was 'til I saw you. You're the bunch that rides for Salem."

"That's right. Now give me a good reason not to kill you before we ride out," Firston said.

"How's this? I think I know where Salem will go now that he's out of the war."

"Why should I care about that? I quit workin' for him when the Yankees swept by here an' took his camp."

"I figured you wrong, I guess," Ben said. "I thought you'd try to get him after what he did to you."

"What do you mean?"

"You rode out to do a job for Salem the night before last. Right?"

"What about it?" Firston asked. He began to sense that Halpert really did know something, but he did not want Halpert to think that his information had any value.

"And the Yankees were waitin' for you when you got there," Ben continued.

"How did you know that?"

"We knew a lot about your group in the camp. News would leak out to the guards an' then to the prisoners. We all knew that you were goin' to get ambushed. Salem set it up that way 'cause he knew he was gettin' out an' he was through with you."

Firston turned back to saddling his horse so Halpert would not see the confusion on his face. It could be just a lie he had made up to save his own skin, but Firston knew that it was just the sort of thing Salem would do.

"Why would Salem want us wiped out?" Firston asked.

" 'Cause if you were captured, you could identify him. He has big plans for after the war, an' he doesn't want any law lookin' for him. He's stolen an' killed a lot during this war, but up 'til now he's always been able to cover his trail up."

Firston thought back to the row of rifles that had spit death at him and his men as they rode up to the Union wagons and of the crossfire they had ridden into as they tried to get away to safety. Somebody had certainly set it up, somebody who knew what route they would take, and somebody who had something to gain by the death of all those men. He wondered why he had not thought of Salem before.

He turned back to Halpert and asked, "All right, where did he go then?"

"If I tell you now, you'll shoot me," Halpert said. "Let me ride with you, an' I'll tell you when we've gotten out of here."

"The hell," Firston said angrily. He struck

the stranger hard in the face with his fist. Halpert went down and did not try to get up. "You'll tell me now!" he stormed. He kicked him hard in the chest.

Halpert writhed in pain, but Firston could tell he was not going to get any information this way. There was pure hatred written on Halpert's face. "You're an amateur," he said. "I've been beaten by experts, an' I know how to take anything you can hand out. Give me a horse, an' I'll tell you a day's ride from here."

Firston looked down at him a moment longer, trying to decide what he wanted to do. Then he said to one of his men, "Cut him loose. He can use Jenkins's horse. Jenkins ain't goin' nowhere. An' get him some clothes."

Starting at dawn they rode hard for several hours, skirting towns and places where there were likely to be troops. Despite his own exhaustion Ben remained doggedly in the saddle and kept up with the gang. He had no idea where they were headed, but he knew they were going west, and that was the direction he wanted to go. But one thing kept troubling him. At the end of the day's ride, when he finally told Firston where Salem had most likely gone, there would be no further use for him, and Firston would probably try to get rid of him.

It would have been easy enough to get separated from the group somewhere along the way, but he wanted Firston to have the information. He wanted this gang to ride to where Salem was and create enough confusion and trouble so that he could sneak in undetected and do his work. There seemed to be only one solution — to get the drop on Firston, to tell him at gunpoint, and then make his escape.

This would be made doubly hard by the fact that Firston and his men were expert gunmen, used to killing men with pistols at close quarters, and Ben had fired a pistol only a few times in his life. He had hunted enough to know his way around rifles well and had even been assigned to a sharp-shooter squad for a while in the army, but he knew that there was an instinct involved in pistol shooting that could only come through practice. But he would have to try, and if a pistol was the only gun he could get his hands on, then he would have to make the best of it.

Firston decided to stop the group for the night at a deserted barn, which stood by the ruins of a burned-out farmhouse. The men were not in very good shape, and Firston knew that some of them would probably drop out of the saddle if they rode on.

He had been thinking all day about what the stranger told him of Salem's double-cross. It all added up just the way Halpert said. Salem would have made plans for after the war. He was too cautious a man not to plan that far ahead, and they would probably be big enough plans that he would not want even the slightest possibility of something from his past coming out to spoil things.

Firston knew that Salem was just as ruthless a man as he himself, but unlike Firston, who was willing to take his own chances and fight his own fights, Salem always had someone else run his risks for him. Even in the prison Salem had his guard, Janson, do his dirty work.

But now Salem had made a mistake, and he was going to pay for it. He had sent Mac Firston and his men riding into a trap, and he was going to pay for that with his life.

They tethered the horses in a grassy spot near the barn where they could graze, and everyone settled down inside the barn. Firston kept his eye on Halpert, who sat down near the door with his back to the wall. Some of the men got out food, which they had thought to bring from the other camp, and passed it around.

One of them gave Halpert something to eat, and he gulped it down ravenously. He watched everyone and everything that went on in the barn, and Firston had the feeling that if anything sudden or threatening happened, he would be out the door instantly and would disappear into the night. It would be better, Firston decided, to get the information he needed now.

He crossed the barn and stood in front of Halpert. "I think you'd better tell me about Salem now, Halpert," he said.

Halpert rose stiffly, and though Firston had faced bigger men, he felt that this man might be one of the toughest if he were pushed too far.

"If you're thinkin' about killin' me as soon as I tell you," Halpert said, "I want to warn you that I'll take a lot of killin'."

Firston knew that everyone in the barn was listening now, and he knew that most of them would not approve of his killing Halpert under these circumstances. They were a rough lot, but most of their kind lived by a loose sort of code of fairness in fighting and killing, and they looked harshly on someone who broke it. He knew that Halpert was not the sort of man who would follow his leadership and that he should be disposed of, but there would be a better time and place for it.

"I haven't got nothin' against you, Halpert," Firston answered. "Just tell us where Salem has gone an' then you can ride out or if you're of a mind, you can stay with us an' help go after him."

"All right," said Halpert. He relaxed somewhat and sat back down. Firston sat down nearby and began to make a cigarette as he listened.

"Like I said," Halpert began, "the prisoners knew a lot about you men. Salem had some of the guards an' a couple of trusted prisoners in on the operation, too, stealin' supplies an' such for you, so it would have been pretty hard for him to cover up the whole business from us. We knew about his plans to get all of you killed, too, but none of us could have gotten word to you even if we had wanted to.

"There were a lot of rumors around about the things Salem did, an' one time or another he had stolen money or personal things from most of us. Word had it that all the money he got from you an' stole from us he sent to his brother out West somewhere. There was never anyone who could say for a fact that he knew it was true, but we all believed it.

"Then one day I was carryin' the trash out of his office to burn it, an' a letter caught my attention. I noticed it 'cause it was from Colorado Territory, an' when I saw that it was from someone named Salem, I stuffed it inside my shirt.

"Later on, when I had a chance to read it, I found out it was from the brother we all heard he had. The brother was tellin' him in the letter that the small ranchers in the area were givin' him a lot of trouble an' that a range war was about to break out. He said he was hirin' gun hands an' gettin' ready for a big fight.

"After I read that I knew that must be where Salem would go when he stopped makin' so much money from the war."

"What's the name of the town?" Firston asked.

"Trinity Wells. Salem's ranch is called the Running S."

No one in the barn spoke for a moment, then Firston said, "Well, boys. I guess I'll be headin' out to Colorado Territory. Any of you think you might like to ride along?"

One of the riders said, "I'd been ridin' with Charley Wilson for three years now, an' I saw him shot out of the saddle back there before he even had a chance to clear leather. I reckon I'd like a crack at the man that laid ol' Charley low."

One by one the other riders began to agree to go along with Firston. When someone double-crossed men like this, he could only expect to face a deadly attempt at revenge if it did not work.

Firston told them they would be moving out at first light, and the men began settling down in various places inside and outside the barn for some badly needed rest.

Ben wandered outside toward the ruins of the farmhouse. The barn and house had been built about fifty yards apart. The walls of the house were stone, and the building had once had a wooden roof, but the roof was burned off, and the walls were tumbling down now, a casualty of the war. The only part of the ruins that remained completely intact was the large stone fireplace.

Ben disliked the thought of sleeping near so many men he could not trust, but he knew he would have no chance of keeping up the next day unless he rested now. So he chose a place in the old house completely away from the rest of the group. He found a spot in one corner and gathered up several stones from the broken-down wall around him. He knew he could not keep anyone from coming up to him, but he thought that if he made the way difficult, he might have a chance of hearing them and defending himself instead of simply being killed as he slept.

Then, after he had taken all the precautions he could, he lay down and slept, leaving his future to fate. Another man might have worried more about the hostile men nearby, but Ben had already known far too many nights of not knowing whether he would live until morning. He knew that keeping his body as fit and strong as possible was as vital a precaution as any other for a man who wanted to stay alive.

CHAPTER FOUR

After he was sure that all the men were asleep, Firston rolled out of his blankets and rose slowly to his feet. He stood still for a moment to make sure that no one had wakened and noticed him, then started quietly over to where he had seen Jim Parry spread his blankets.

Parry was a sort of second-in-command when Firston needed one. He had sometimes led small raids when Firston was busy with something else, and he also followed Firston's orders completely. He was too loyal, and too dumb, to ever question any of Firston's decisions. Firston had been the first man to ever give Parry the chance to stand out from a group of men, and Parry was absolutely devoted to him because of it. Firston often used Parry on small jobs that he did not want anyone to know about or that required a man who was unswervingly obedient.

When he reached Parry, Firston nudged him with his foot and motioned for him to step outside. The night was pitch black, and they could see only a few feet ahead of them. It was perfect for Firston's purpose.

Only when they were several yards away from the barn did Firston stop. He turned to Parry and said, "I don't like the looks of this new man. I don't think he'd be reliable in a pinch. He wouldn't follow orders."

Parry nodded his head solemnly to everything Firston said. Firston continued, "I think we'd better get rid of him now. I saw him head off to that house to sleep. We can ease in there an' do our work with a knife an' then dump his body in that creek down the hill. In the mornin' everyone will just think he left during the night." Though Firston was saying "we," it was understood that the task was being assigned to Parry.

"Sure, Mac," Parry said. "I can take care of him . . . no trouble a'tall." He drew a long bowie knife from his belt sheath and tested the edge with his thumb.

Firston grinned at Parry's willingness to do the job. He had seen Parry handle a knife many times and knew he was good. "All right, Jim," he said. "Come an' get me when it's done, an' I'll help you carry him off."

Parry crept off silently and in a moment

was visible only as a vague outline against the stone of one of the crumbling walls of the house. Then, as quietly as a cat, he rounded the edge of the chimney and was out of sight.

It was a few minutes before Firston was rewarded by the sound of a thud and a quick low moan. As he started forward he heard the sound of low voices inside the ruins. Someone must have come out of the barn and caught Parry in the act, but Firston knew he could lie or threaten his way out of it, or simply kill whomever it was.

Drawing his gun he went the way Parry had gone, around the chimney and into the ruins. A few feet in front of him two men were standing over the body of a third. "At least he got the job done before he was caught," Firston thought, but as he approached he realized that it was Parry who was down.

Both of the standing men had revolvers in their hands. When they saw Firston approach, one of them said, "I'm glad you're here, boss. Saves me the trouble of comin' to get you."

The speaker was Ridge Parkman, one of the newer members of the gang. He had joined only a few months before, and Firston knew very little about him.

"Ol' Parry here must have gone crazy," Parkman continued. "I was sleepin' over there by the chimney when he come slippin' by with that knife in his hand. He was headed right for this new fella.

"Wal, I thought I would rap him across the head where we could tie him up an' talk some sense into him, but I guess he fell on his knife."

The other man was Halpert. His low bitter voice cut through the darkness to Firston. "He might have been put up to this by someone."

Firston saw that Halpert held Parry's gun, and that it was pointed at him.

"Couldn't be," Parkman drawled. "Mr. Firston is the only one that Parry took orders from, an' he already said tonight that he didn't have nothin' against you. Isn't that right, Mr. Firston?"

"That's right," Firston said.

"I heard him say it," Halpert said.

"Ol' Parry must of just got a wild notion," Parkman said.

"Well, whoever caused it, I'm riding out," Halpert said. "I don't think I could rest peaceful around this bunch again."

"I think that's a wise idea," Firston said. "An' maybe you should ride out with him, Parkman. Parry was pretty well liked by

36

some of the boys."

"You got a point, boss," Parkman agreed. "Somebody might not understand, Parry failin' on his knife an' all. I've been thinkin' I might try going straight for a while anyway. I used to be a pretty good cow puncher 'fore I got into this outlaw business."

"You can take the horse you rode here on, Halpert."

"An' he might as well take Parry's gun and holster, boss. It's a cinch Parry ain't needin' 'em now."

"All right, but ride far, you two. Next time we meet I might have forgotten that Parry just fell on his own knife."

By dusk the next day the two men were many miles west of Firston's camp. They stopped to rest in a small depression sheltered by some trees where they could watch most of the open country around them without being seen.

As Parkman was putting together a few sticks for a small cooking fire, Ben said, "I'm obliged to you for your help back there, but I don't see why you did it. Those men were your friends, an' I'm a stranger."

"You're wrong there," Parkman said. "I didn't have one friend in the lot of them. Especially Parry. He an' I didn't get on too well. I didn't like the way he killed."

"What were you doing with them? You don't seem like the type for that kind of lousy business."

"I needed the money, an' it didn't seem so bad when I joined up. I didn't get the full picture 'til later."

"Why didn't you leave then?"

"I wouldn't have made it ten miles. Firston don't like quitters. He'd have got me, so I stayed. Last night was different, an' I'm glad we got the drop on him before he knew what was happening."

"It still seems like there's more to this than it looks like. Where did you come from back there? You weren't sleeping by the chimney like you told Firston. I was the only one in the ruins of that house."

"I was outside the barn," Parkman said. "When I threw in with that bunch I got in the habit of bedding down away from where most of the men were at night.

"I heard Firston an' Parry come out of the barn, an' I heard 'em talkin' about gettin' rid of you. I guess it just stuck in my craw, so I circled around an' got to Parry before he reached you. I owed Parry one anyway. He got likkered up one night an' used that hog skinner on a pard of mine."

"Well, I'm obliged, whatever your reasons were."

Parkman had spread his bedroll out near the fire, and Ben watched as he laid his gun belt beside his head and checked to make sure the six-shooter was within easy reach when he lay down. After finding himself a place to sleep, Ben did the same with the gun belt he had. Full of the beans and salt pork that Parkman had cooked, he fell into the first peaceful sleep he had known in some time.

Ben woke at dawn to the smell of coffee boiling on a small fire. He raised up and looked over toward where Parkman had slept, but his bedroll was already rolled up, and the gun belt and the man were gone. Ben got himself a cup of coffee and sat back against a tree to enjoy the sheer luxury of it.

From the time of his escape until this moment there had been no time and too much danger to really realize that he was free. He did not have to rub his ankles because he had slept shackled to an iron ring in the floor. He had not been wakened by a boot in his ribs. He could get up and walk around, talk, sing, come or go . . . he was a free man, and in one solemn moment he resolved that no man would ever take that freedom away from him again.

And there was real coffee. Ben had almost forgotten what it tasted like. In prison they had been given chicory, and sometimes just boiled bark, instead of coffee . . . but now here was a whole pot in front of him.

Parkman came back in a few minutes. As he poured himself a steaming cup of the coffee, he explained where he had been.

"I thought Firston might have second thoughts about lettin' us leave like that, so I did a little scouting. Like I said, he's not normally a man to leave loose ends, but I guess he's gettin' careless, or else he's too interested in gettin' away himself to worry about us. Anyway, there's not been nobody else come near this place since we got here."

"That's good news," Ben said. "If it came to a scrap, I don't know how much use I would be to you with this thing." He patted the six-gun beside him. He had strapped it on, but it felt cumbersome and strange there on his leg. "I've never shot one a dozen times."

"That don't exactly make you an expert at it," Parkman agreed.

"Nope. I passed a good bit of time in close company with a rifle, though."

"Well," Parkman said. "That'll help when I start teachin' you about that leg iron. At least you'll know how to aim, but I guess you'll have to learn to draw from scratch."

Ben sat up at these words. "I wasn't hintin' for no lessons," he said. "I figured on tradin' this thing somewhere for a rifle first chance I got."

"Yeah," Parkman speculated. "A rifle's all right for some things, but if you happen to go up against a man who can do this . . ." In a flash Parkman's pistol was in his hand, and the gaping end of its barrel pointing straight at Ben drove the rest of Parkman's words home. ". . . then that rifle's no more use than a chunk of firewood." He reholstered the gun, picked up a stick, and began poking some life into the dying fire. He pitched a few sticks on the flames and then sliced some salt pork into a skillet and put it on the fire to cook.

Ben watched him and thought about what he had said. The lightning draw he had just seen was a pretty effective argument for learning to use a pistol. He had always thought that when he did finally get the chance to go after Salem, he would get him with guts and brains, but now he was beginning to think that maybe he should learn a few things before he made his try. If learning to use a six-gun was what it took, he'd have to learn and practice until he was better than anyone who might stand in his way.

"I'd appreciate you teachin' me I guess," Ben said, "but I think you'll change your mind when you hear where I aim to go."

"I don't s'pose the place would be Trinity Wells, would it?" Parkman asked.

"I guess it is," Ben said.

Parkman continued to cook the pork and did not look up at Ben. "It shapes up," he said, "like things is goin' to get pretty hot down around those parts. Guess a man would be a damn fool to ride into something like that if he had no part in it."

When the pork was cooked they sat and ate it in silence. Ben took Parkman's words to mean that they would soon be parting trails. He regretted the fact because he truly liked Parkman and felt that there was a lot he could learn from him, but he agreed that steering clear of Trinity Wells was the wisest choice for Parkman.

After they finished eating it took them only a few minutes to gather up their belongings and saddle the horses. When Ben mounted up and turned his horse west, he half expected Parkman to turn and ride out in another direction. Instead he caught up with Ben and rode alongside as they headed up out of the draw and across the open meadow. Ben still did not speak, but the question hung in the air, and he was itching to ask it.

Parkman must have sensed his thoughts, for after they had ridden for a few minutes, he drawled, almost as if he were talking to himself, "Pappy always said I was long on spunk and short on brains. Those words are ringin' pretty true right about now. I reckon if we ride north of here a ways, we'll pick up the best trail west to Colorado Territory."

CHAPTER FIVE

It had been some time since Ben had had the leisure to consider such abstracts as friendship. In the world he had just come from, a man could count on no one except himself, could trust no one but himself, and worried about no one but himself. You might trust someone only to have him betray you for an extra share of food. You might help someone one minute and the next find him trying to steal from you. It was a hard world, and Ben had been thoroughly conditioned to it.

That was one reason why he had so much trouble accepting the open friendship of Ridge Parkman. In the system Ben was used to, it was necessary to be instantly suspicious of anyone who did something for you. The price they demanded in repayment was usually too high.

But as the days passed Ben started to realize that it really was not that way with

Parkman. Since the time Parkman had saved Ben's life and taken him under his wing, they had lived off Parkman's dwindling bankroll because Ben had no money, and Parkman had taught Ben many things that he would need to know to live in this western country that they were entering. And he had never showed in any way that he expected anything in return.

And true to his word, Parkman began teaching Ben how to handle a six-gun. Before he met Parkman Ben had just assumed that it was all a matter of getting the gun out of the holster and firing it. And truly it was, but as he progressed he began to realize that the refinements of those two simple acts, of drawing and firing, could very easily mean the difference between living and dying in a gunfight.

Every day as they rode Ben practiced until his arm was so tired that the gun felt like it weighed fifty pounds. But each day it took longer for the gun to get heavy, and each day it slid out of the holster more like Parkman's had done that first day. Parkman also taught him about instinct shooting and about how to move and dodge as he fired.

He told Ben that he was really a cowboy by profession, but his knowledge of guns and gun handling belied the fact. Besides that, Parkman had just come from a world that demanded a fast gun to stay alive, and he was riding into a situation that looked to be a shooting range war. Neither place would be where an ordinary cowboy would want to go. Ben wondered about who Parkman might really be, but he let his question go unasked.

Most of the country they rode through was Union controlled. When they were stopped and questioned they always professed to be cowboys returning from driving a small herd of cattle to the army, and as they got farther west, the patrols they met were fewer. Most of the fighting was far east of them, and the soldiers they met were not so tense and suspicious as those in the East had been.

Finally, far out in Kansas, the questioning and suspicion stopped entirely. At last they were in country where a man on horseback wearing plain working clothes and a gun was just naturally assumed to be a cowboy.

In western Kansas they turned south for a while. Trinity Wells was in the southern part of Colorado Territory, out of the gold country and therefore out of the mainstream of the bustling growth of the area. The country they were riding through was flat and dry, and Ben could only imagine what the trip would have been like without a trail-wise companion like Parkman along. As they crossed over into the parched country of southeast Colorado, Parkman's poke began to run low. They ate jack rabbits and spent many hours cleaning out barns and doing odd jobs for a free meal at the small ranches along the way.

Parkman wanted to stop and work a while to put together a few dollars, but Ben rejected the idea for himself. He was too close to Salem now, and Parkman understood his eagerness well enough to give in to his wishes.

As they rode west, now close to their objective, Ben was more eager to start riding in the morning and more reluctant to stop at night. Parkman remembered having been in Trinity Wells once a few years before, and each night Ben went over with him again everything he knew about the town.

It was small as Parkman remembered it, and very peaceful back then. The town itself was at the mouth of a wide valley, almost like a cork in a bottle. The ranches that dotted the valley were all small spreads, and Parkman said he remembered thinking then how odd it was that nobody anywhere around had gotten greedy ideas of taking over everything. He said the valley struck him as being ideally suited for one large spread. With natural barriers on three sides of the valley, one spread could be maintained with a minimum of hands. Big profits could be made fast. But as it was set up now, each small ranch had to keep several hands to prevent the cattle from the various ranches from mingling and scattering.

Ben knew very little about the cattle business, of the rules that governed how a man might acquire grazing land, cattle, and a foothold in the business, but judging from Parkman's analysis, he guessed he knew what Salem and his brother were trying to do in the Trinity Wells area. If there was good money to be made from taking over the whole area, then that was probably their objective; and if all the other ranches were as small as they had been when Parkman was last there, then Salem's chances of success seemed pretty good.

But gazing deep into the evening campfire, Ben unconsciously set his jaw. He swore to himself that Salem would never live long enough to enjoy any success in the cattle business or any other enterprise. They were just a day's ride from Trinity Wells now, and Salem's days were numbered. His hours were numbered.

Parkman's whisper broke into Ben's reverie. Ben looked up to see the other man with his gun already in his hand, looking anxiously out into the darkness. "Douse that fire," Parkman hissed. "We've got company out there somewhere."

Ben leaned forward and quickly poured the contents of the coffee pot over the small fire. With a hissing rush of steam the flames died, and the small clearing was swallowed up in darkness. Ben turned and, crouching low on the other side of the clearing from Parkman, drew his gun and strained to see out into the surrounding brush. With a pulse of anxiety he realized that he had broken one of Parkman's most important rules. Never gaze long into a fire. It makes a man night blind.

Now Ben knew exactly what Parkman had meant, and now it might be too late. It would take him several minutes to adjust his eyes to the darkness, but before that much time passed he might be dead. But at least he had the revolver, and it felt familiar and reassuring in his hand now, not strange like it had that first night when he picked it up and pointed it at Firston.

"What is it?" Ben whispered.

"Somebody moved out from behind a tree about thirty feet away over there an' outlined himself against the sky for a second. An' then the brush rustled off to the left. Didn't you hear it?"

Ben did not answer, but sheepishly admitted to himself that he had been so lost in his own thoughts that he had not seen or heard anything. That was two mistakes he had made tonight, and either could have cost him his life.

"Don't be too quick on the trigger," Parkman advised. "We don't know who it is. Maybe they're friendly."

There was a rustling in the brush on one side of them, and a man's voice growled out low, "Damn, Joe! Get over there where I told you. I'm liable to shoot you by mistake if you keep inchin' in on me like that!"

"Well, where are they, Sy?" another voice asked. "I can't see their fire anymore."

"They've put it out," the growly voice answered. "Now shut up before they hear us."

Ben realized that the two men must have been coming through the heavy brush on that side and probably did not know how close to the camp they already were. Suddenly Parkman spoke up, "We hear you now," he challenged. "What do you want?" Ben could vaguely see Parkman moving away from the place he had been when he spoke. If anyone fired at the sound of his voice, he would not be there.

And someone did fire. The explosion rang out startlingly close, and a bullet furrowed the ground between Ben and Parkman. Ben tensed, but Parkman waved for him not to fire. Almost immediately following the sound of the shot there was the loud smack of a fist striking flesh and the unmistakable thud of someone falling to the ground.

Then the gruffer of the two voices in the darkness spoke up. "That shot was a mistake," the man said. "We mean to give you a chance to give up peaceable-like, but you're surrounded, an' we'll shoot you if we have to."

"Give up to who?" It was Ben who spoke this time, and he too changed his position immediately after.

"We're a posse," the gruff voice said. "I'm the sheriff of Trinity Wells, an' we want to ask you boys a few questions."

There was a moment of silence during which Ben gazed across the clearing at Parkman. Parkman gave an exaggerated shrug of his shoulders and then turned back to covering the trees with his pistol.

"Don't get any foolish notions," the voice in the brush continued, "like tryin' to make a break for it. Like I said, you're surrounded." Then a little louder he said, "You men on the other side. Let 'em know you're there."

In confirmation the brush rustled in a couple of places around Ben and Parkman, a couple of men spoke up, and there was the sound of shotgun hammers being cocked. Crouching low, Parkman crossed the clearing to Ben's side. "Sounds like there's a passel of 'em," Parkman whispered.

"Do you think they're really the law?" Ben asked.

"I figure they might be," Parkman answered. "They could've opened up by now if they just wanted to get rid of us."

"I'll leave it up to you," Ben whispered. "I'm with you either way."

Parkman nodded his head solemnly and then stood up. "Come on in," he called out to the darkness.

There was a rustling in the bushes all around as the captors moved in closer. To Ben it sounded like an army on the move. In a minute a tall form appeared at the edge of the clearing. Ben could make out the glisten of moonlight on the man's badge and on his raised gun barrel.

Ben stood up beside Parkman, and both of them waited with their guns pointed at the intruder.

"Better play it our way, boys," the man said calmly. "You've got nothin' to lose if you're not the men we're lookin' for."

"You're dealin'," Parkman said suspiciously.

"All right," the man said. "Put 'em there on the ground an' then back away. Move slowly an' don't get in front of one another."

Ben cast a quick sideways glance at Parkman and then returned his gaze to the stranger. Parkman waited a moment longer and then laid his gun on the ground and moved away from it. Ben did the same, and the man walked over until he was standing directly over the two guns. "All right, you men," he called out to the darkness. "Come on in. I've got 'em."

From all around the edge of the clearing men started coming out of the brush until six others had joined the man who covered Ben and Parkman.

"Build up a fire, somebody," the tall man ordered. One of the newcomers bolstered his gun and started piling the wood Ben had gathered to cook with onto the fire. Two others went into the edge of the trees and gathered more wood to add to the supply. All four of the others kept their guns on the two prisoners.

As the light from the fire grew, Ben began to examine the "posse." The tall man with the badge who had first come out of the shadows had a look of integrity that added to his claim of being a lawman. He was about fifty, with gray hair showing at his temples under the brim of his hat, but his build and carriage showed no indication that he might be past his prime. His long mustache drooped down past a mouth set in a firm, determined line, but his eyes showed fairness.

The other man who had come out of the bushes from the same direction as the sheriff, and evidently the one to whom the sheriff had been talking, was a lot younger. He was shorter than the sheriff and had a slim build. His clothes though western, were new and showed little wear. His boots were shiny, and his new, white Stetson was set back on his head at a jaunty angle. As he came up next to the sheriff he was rubbing his jaw. "You had no reason to hit me like that, Sy," he said.

"You could of gotten somebody hurt, flying off the handle like that, Joe," the sheriff said sternly. "If these two had opened up, we'd of had to nail them without gettin' even a look at them."

"Well, we didn't come all the way out here

to shake their hands," Joe said indignantly.

"We don't know a thing about these two," the sheriff said. "They might not be the ones."

"Well, they certainly look like the type," Joe said with a sneer. "Don't they look like the ones, dad?"

The man Joe addressed had been lagging back, and only now did he come cautiously forward to get a look at Ben and Parkman. In dress and temperament, he looked completely unsuited to be riding with a posse. He wore town clothes — a suit, round bowler, and low-cut shoes. He appeared to be no older than the sheriff, but his soft, untanned hands and paunchy stomach attested to the fact that he did not live nearly as active a life. He acted embarrassed at having to look at the two captives as they stared down at him, but he surveyed them both from a safe distance.

"What about it, Mr. Guthrie?" the sheriff asked impatiently. "Are these the jaspers?"

"Well . . ." the little man hesitated. "They were wearing masks. . . ."

Parkman evidently had grown tired of the suspense and now addressed the sheriff directly. "What have the men you're huntin' for done?"

"They stuck up the bank in Trinity Wells

55

Thursday. . . ." the sheriff began.

"That was my dad's bank," Joe interrupted. "And we want that money back right now." He advanced toward the two prisoners with what was supposed to be a menacing wave of his gun.

"Dammit, Joe!" the sheriff said angrily. "Now you put that thing in its holster an' don't take it out again unless I tell you to!"

Joe holstered his gun indignantly and turned away to face the fire. "You've got to be tough with their kind," he mumbled, "or you won't ever get anything from them."

"If this dude saw the holdup," Parkman continued calmly, indicating the man in the suit, "then he should be able to tell you straight off that we're not the ones. Three days ago on Thursday we were a hundred miles east of here, an' that's probably where the men you're lookin' for are right now. They'd be stupid to hole up right here in your back yard."

"They could of holed up here thinkin' we would ride right past 'em, Sy," one of the other men reasoned. He and the other three members of the posse were all middle-aged, substantial-looking men, but still they appeared to be true frontiersmen and formidable opponents with guns in their hands.

"You told us you would know the men if

you saw them again," the sheriff said. "Do you recognize these two?"

"They were masked, don't forget," Guthrie stalled. "And there were three of them, not two. . . ."

"We all know they could have split up," the sheriff explained patiently.

"You could search us," Ben suggested. "We haven't got but six or seven dollars between us. That ought to prove somethin'."

"I reckon we should," the sheriff said. He instructed Ben and Parkman to empty their pockets and designated two members of the posse to search the saddlebags and look around the camp area. No money was found except the few dollars Ben had mentioned.

"They could have it hidden anywhere," Joe said indignantly.

"Could be," the sheriff said. The whole time he had been studying them, and something in his expression began to show that he did not believe they were the robbers. "I guess you boys will have to ride to town with us 'til we can get this thing cleared up."

"You're just goin' to stop lookin' 'cause you have us?" Ben asked.

"We've been lookin' for two days," the sheriff said. "We'd already given up an' was on our way back to town when we caught a glimpse of your fire."

"We were ridin' toward Trinity Wells anyway," Parkman said. "Might as well go in style."

CHAPTER SIX

The posse camped there that night with two men awake at all times to guard Ben and Parkman. Joe had wanted to tie them to trees, but the sheriff rejected the idea as unnecessary. At first light they were on the trail, and by noon they were entering the edge of Trinity Wells.

Parkman told Ben that the town had not changed much, and Ben could see that it was much the same as Parkman had described it to him on the trail.

The one long, main street was dominated by false-front buildings. There were four saloons and an assortment of dry goods stores, cafés, and the general suppliers of the needs of ranchers and cowboys. The big barn of the town livery stable and a town meeting hall were at the opposite end of town. Near the center of town Parkman leaned over in his saddle toward the retiring Mr. Guthrie and, indicating a two-story yellow building with no sign on the front, asked, "Is that still Miss Paula's Palace?"

The banker flushed several shades of crimson and said, "I have no knowledge of the affairs of Miss Paula Elliott and her . . . uh . . . female boarders."

"I guess sonny boy over there would know more about that place," Ben drawled to Parkman.

Joe Guthrie, the banker's son, turned in his saddle, and his right hand dropped quickly to the grip of the pistol he wore. But the sheriff, who was riding at the head of the group, turned and gave the young man a serious look, which stopped him from drawing the gun.

As the posse entered the edge of town, people began to come out of the stores and saloons to gaze at the two prisoners, and as they neared the jail about midway down the main street, the group of onlookers, which walked along the sidewalks and followed in the street, had grown larger. It seemed to Ben to be an ill-tempered crowd, too. He caught several remarks from the crowd about what they thought was the best way to deal with bank robbers, and none of the ways had anything to do with a court and a jury.

The sheriff had evidently been overhearing the same talk, because when he reined his horse up at the jail and dismounted, he turned to the crowd and held up his hands for silence.

"Now we got two men here," he said, "but we just come across them out there camped peaceful like, an' we don't know if they've done anythin' or not. You folks have been satisfied with the way I've kept the law for a sight of years, an' I don't see any reason why you should stop now. If these are the jaspers that held up the bank, I'm gonna see that they get what's comin' to them, but I don't want to hear no more talk about stretchin' necks." He turned and started into his office, but a voice from the crowd stopped him.

"That's the men all right, sheriff," a woman's voice said. Ben and Parkman turned to see a small, elderly woman making her way to the front of the crowd. As she neared the group of horsemen, she said, "I recognize that one." She pointed an accusing finger at Ben. "He's got the same killer eyes I saw on one of those masked men in the bank Thursday."

The sheriff turned back and looked down at the woman and then up at Ben. When he spoke there was tolerance and a trace of humor in his voice. "I reckon that gent's eyes ain't no different from most anybody else's, Miss Elviney. You'll get a chance to make a statement later, but I don't want you stirrin' up this crowd with talk like that."

He motioned for the prisoners and posse to get down and go in the office, but as they were doing so, the woman spoke up again, louder and more insistently than before. "Sy Perkins! Now you quit talkin' down to me and listen! I know killer eyes when I see them."

After the entire group had gone in the office, the sheriff turned to the crowd again and said, "Now I don't want the whole town tryin' to pack into my office. You folks that was there in the bank that day come on in an' get a close look at these two, an' the rest of you go on about your business." A few people started forward, and the rest of the crowd began leaving, reluctantly respectful of the sheriff's wishes.

One member of the posse locked Ben and Parkman in one of the two cells that filled the rear of the building. Despite what the sheriff had said about not wanting his office full of people, it quickly filled up as the witnesses came in to join the posse members who were already there. Everybody talked at once, and the general tone of hostility in the room made Ben feel uneasy. He had imagined that they would be cleared as soon as they got to town, but now the witnesses were beginning to convince themselves that they had seen Ben and Parkman in the bank, and the old woman was right in the thick of it all leading the group in accusations. He and Parkman moved to the back of the cell and sat down on one of the bunks for a short conference.

"It don't look so good for us, pardner," Parkman said in a slow, thoughtful drawl.

"I don't like this one bit," Ben said. "Some of these people are really convinced that we're the ones."

"They want us to be the bad guys real bad, but I'll still put my money on that sheriff. I judge him for a fair man with a good head. He wouldn't let things get out of hand without bein' certain that we were guilty."

"I hope you're right," Ben muttered.

Just then the sheriff came to the cell door and said to them, "You two come over here so's these folks can get a close look at you."

They rose and went to the front of the cell. The witnesses crowded close and began to discuss their characteristics, much the same as people might discuss a pair of horses in a corral. A couple of the witnesses were convinced that Ben and Parkman were the robbers, but most of the rest of them were unsure. Nobody immediately stated the conviction that they were not.

Ben, in turn, examined each one of the witnesses, his glance going from face to face, his eyes meeting those of the townspeople defiantly. At the other side of the room near the door his glance stopped on one certain person. It was a girl of about twenty. She was dressed in riding pants and a colored blouse. Her western hat rested atop a head of flowing auburn hair, and her face, frowning slightly in thoughtfulness, struck Ben as one of the prettiest he had seen in a long while. Even as he watched her, their eyes met, and Ben noticed that there was no suspicion or resentment in her gaze. Ben tried to hold her eyes, but in a moment she shifted them to Parkman.

The confusion continued for a few minutes longer. Off to one side the sheriff was busy collecting rifles from the members of the posse and putting them in a rack behind his desk. One by one the posse members, with the exception of the banker and his son, went out and left the small office area a little less crowded.

When the collecting of the rifles was finished, the sheriff came to the door of the cell and said to the people in the room. "Well, I reckon you've all had a good enough look. I'll start takin' your statements now."

It was then that the girl in the back spoke up. "You don't need to bother, sheriff," she said. Something in her tone made everyone else stop talking and listen to her. "Neither of these men are the ones who robbed the bank."

"Now that's mighty interestin', Miss Clarice," the sheriff said, "but how can you be so sure?"

Joe Guthrie moved to the girl's side and took her arm gently as she spoke. He tried to ease her around toward the door as he said, "Let's leave this to the sheriff and these other people, Clarice. They'll know how to take care of these rascals."

"But they aren't the men, Joe," she said calmly. She pulled her arm free of his grasp and advanced through the group toward the cell. "None of the men had hair as long as this man's," she said, pointing to Ben. "And this other one," she said, indicating Parkman, "is two or three inches too tall to be any one of the three robbers. It's really very simple."

"Wal, I guess that's right, Sy," one of the other witnesses said. He was a man of about forty, dressed in work clothes and wearing a gun belt. "I reckon we was in such a hurry to get us some bad men and get our money back that we just didn't stop to think."

"Can any of the rest of you say for a fact that what Miss Clarice has said ain't so?" the sheriff asked.

"It's the same killer eyes," Miss Elviney said. "I oughta know killer eyes when I see them." But nobody was paying any attention to her now as they considered and began to agree with what the girl had said.

Joe Guthrie had moved to the girl's side again and was whispering angrily to her. In a moment she pulled her arm free for a second time and said to him, "I'll not be treated like a child, Joe! I was in the bank that day just the same as the rest of these people, and I saw as much as they did. I don't understand why you're so anxious to see innocent men kept in jail!"

Joe took a halting step backward, recoiling from her outburst and embarrassed that there were so many witnesses to her defiance. When he answered her his voice was hurt and defensive. "I just think they should be kept here 'til we're sure."

Still angry, Clarice turned away from him without answering and said to the sheriff, "I'm positive that these aren't the men, sheriff. I'd like for you to have the real bank robbers in jail as much as anybody. My dad had money in the bank, and he will be hurt right along with everybody else, but if you don't have the right men, you don't have them. It's your duty to let them out."

"It's lookin' more that way, Miss Clarice," the sheriff answered. "What do the rest of you folks say? Can any of you say for sure that you recognize these men?" Then, with a glance at Miss Elviney, he added, "Recognize the whole man, that is, an' not just his eyes?"

"I'm for lettin' 'em go," the man in work clothes said. "We got no evidence, none a'tall."

"An' how about you, Mr. Guthrie?" the sheriff asked.

The banker squirmed at the attention that the sheriff's question brought him. "Well, Sy . . ." he stuttered, "I guess . . . and the masks . . . probably Miss Clarice . . . I don't see . . ."

"You think we ought to let them go, then?" the sheriff prompted.

The banker nodded his head and, muttering inaudibly, backed toward the corner where he had been standing most of the time. Joe watched his father uncertainly and with some disdain, and when he saw that the elderly banker was going along with everyone else, he threw up his hands in frustration and stomped from the office.

The sheriff watched the young man's performance with a frown on his face, and when Joe had gone out the door, he turned to the banker and said sternly, "Reckon that boy ain't too old to wallop. You might even find one or two folks around town that would help."

"It's a fact," the man in work clothes said.

"He's a constant worry," the banker said sadly. "He's such a headstrong young man."

"Bullheaded is more like it," Clarice said.

The sheriff turned to her and, with a teasing grin on his face, asked, "If you feel like that, Miss Clarice, then why are you fixin' to get hitched to him?"

Blushing furiously, and suddenly very shy, she answered meekly, "He's got his good side, too. He can be very nice when he wants to."

"If you say so, ma'am," Parkman said. Everybody looked quickly at him, surprised that one of the men behind the bars had butted in on the conversation. "But I'd rather hear about it," he continued, "after the sheriff has put the key into this here door."

"Guess you're right there, mister," the

sheriff said with a grin. He picked up the keys to the cell and went over to open the door. The townspeople had begun to leave the office, and by the time the sheriff had returned Ben and Parkman's gun belts, almost everyone was gone. Only the middle-aged man in work clothes remained. He waited by the door, and as Ben and Parkman were starting out, he said, "I'd like to buy you boys a beer if you're willin'. I reckon there shouldn't be any hard feelin's amongst us over this business of bein' mistook for bank robbers."

"Suits me," Parkman said with a grin. "I'm plumb dry." He turned his head and looked at Ben.

"Sure," Ben said, but he had no smiles to waste on strangers. The three of them left the jail and walked diagonally across the street to Slater's Saloon.

Several men were leaning against the bar, drinking and talking. Three of the four tables in the middle of the room were taken. The man led his two companions to the empty one.

"Reckon I ought to introduce myself," the man said. "The name's Paulson. I own one of the small spreads up in the valley."

"Ridge Parkman," Parkman said. "Glad to meetcha. And this here's Ben Halpert."

They shook hands around, and the bartender came to the table to take their order. He scowled at Ben and Parkman and then looked questioningly at Paulson. He had evidently seen the posse bring them in and could not figure out why they were out of the jail.

"Sy let these gents go," Paulson said in answer to the bartender's unspoken question. "We figured out, us that was in the bank that day, that it wasn't them."

"For certain?" the bartender asked suspiciously.

"The onliest ones who doubted it was Miss Elviney . . ." he paused and gave the bartender a significant wink, ". . . an' young Joe Guthrie. An' he wasn't even there."

The bartender grunted and turned away to get the pitcher of beer they ordered.

"I can't figure it," Parkman said. "Why does everybody want so powerful for us to be the bank robbers? Is this town hungry for a hangin' or what?"

"No, not that so much," Paulson answered. "It's just that the holdup, comin' when it did, kinda knocked this town an' the small ranchers hereabouts to their knees. See, ol' Arthur Guthrie, the bank president, is a kind man, an' that makes him a terrible bank president. Over the last few years we've had some lean times up in the valley, an' he's kept several of the smaller spreads goin' with second and third mortgages an' loans that he knows he'll never get back. So a couple of months ago when the board met, they found out that the bank was gone broke.

"Then is when Joe Guthrie come up with this big idea. He had jus' got back from studyin' business back East, an' I guess those fellers filled his head full of notions about takin' risks and makin' big money an' such. Well, he said we could cancel the insurance on the bank's money for about three months an' take the money that the insurance cost an' use it to get the bank back on its feet. We knowed it was a risk, but we voted to try it, an' we decided to keep it a secret so people wouldn't lose confidence in the bank an' pull their money out.

"An' it worked fine for a while. We were beginnin' to see daylight, an' Arthur Guthrie said he thought he could save the bank, but that was before last Thursday an' the holdup."

"What's all that mean in regular talk?" Ben asked.

"It means that all the people that had money in the bank have lost it, just the same

as if they had buried it in a can an' somebody else had come along and dug it up."

"So maybe that's why the boy was so
strong on keepin' Ben an' me behind bars,"
Parkman speculated. "It was his idea that
put everybody up a crick, an' he's hankerin'
bad to see some fingers pointed in some
other direction besides his."

"Somethin' like that," Paulson agreed.
"An' I guess maybe you fellas should know
that there will be a lots of folks that won't
have no more use for you two than Joe does.
The smart thing would probably just be to
pull out for fur parts."

"We ain't," Ben said shortly.

"No sir," Parkman agreed, somewhat
more amiably. "We figgered on stickin' here
for a while."

Paulson's face clouded, and he eyed the
two as if he were just then seeing them for
the first time. "If you two is hired guns an'
figgerin' on joinin' that Salem bunch, I figger you need a warnin' about that, too." His
voice had lost all its friendliness, and Parkman recognized the signs of a man tensed
for sudden violence.

"We ain't for hire," Parkman said, and his
grin did much to relax the older man.

"But what about Salem?" Ben asked, suddenly more interested in the talk.

"You know 'im?" Paulson asked.

"Just heard tell."

"Then you know he's the skunk that's tryin' to take over the valley. Wasn't so bad when it was just Jude Salem here. He come in and bought the Smith spread at the upper end of the valley. Folks hereabouts made him welcome, an' he didn't crowd nobody right off. Then after a while he commenced to buyin' bits an' pieces of land all over the valley, an' folks started wonderin' why he wanted to get hisself so scattered out for.

"Then a couple of months ago Jude's brother, Lester, got here. That's a hard man, that Lester, more of a driver than his brother. He started makin' folks offers for their spreads, not decent offers, mind, but always too little, an' when they turned him down, stuff started happenin' to them. Barns would catch fire all by themselves, an' bunches of cattle would disappear or be found layin' dead somewheres. Nothin' could be proved, but some folks started takin' the hint an' sellin'.

"There's still a lot of us holdin' out, but most of us are feelin' the squeeze. Reckon somethin's gonna have to be done about Salem, but he's got a gang of tough hombres ridin' for him. An' now with this bank deal, there's not much cash amongst the rest of us to hire the men it would take to stand up to him."

"Where's Salem?" Ben asked bluntly.

"Well, now, if you wasn't aimin' to join up with him," Paulson asked solemnly, "I can't see why you'd need that information."

"Guess it'd be a good idea to know where to stay away from," Parkman reasoned.

"That'd be smart," the rancher said suspiciously. "This road you come in on goes west right up the middle of the valley. Salem's spread is the Running S, an' it's the last one before the road turns into a trail an' starts up into the mountains. He an' his brother got them a big house out there. It's like a fortress from what I hear. An' they're not too keen on visitors."

"It don't sound like a place I'd want to visit anyway," Parkman commented.

Parkman and Paulson continued to make small talk until the pitcher of beer was gone. When Ben drained the last of the beer from his glass, he stood up and said, "Better be goin'." He turned without further comment and started toward the door.

As Parkman rose to follow, Paulson said, "That Halpert is a mighty savin' man with words."

"He is for a fact," Parkman agreed. "Good talkin' to you," he said, and then added with a grin, "an' good drinkin' your beer."

"Guess I'll see you around town," Paulson said.

"We'll be here. Lookin' for work."

Parkman left the saloon and crossed the street to where Ben was checking the cinch on his saddle. He walked up to Ben and took ahold of his arm as if to hold him back. "I know what you're figgerin' to do," he drawled, "an' it ain't smart."

"Don't see any need of puttin' it off," Ben said. He finished adjusting the saddle and prepared to mount.

"What do you figger to do, just ride in calmly an plug him an' ride out?"

"I'll work it out when I get there."

"What about all them gun hands he's got, an' that fort house?"

"Don't know yet."

"There's ways to get a man an' live through it your own self, but you've got to plan it a little. I came here to help you, an' I will, 'less you figger you've done learned everything useful I can teach you."

Ben had been standing with his back partly turned to Parkman, his stance stiff and determined. He turned now, and his eyes met Parkman's squarely. "It's eatin' at me, Ridge," he said. "I've gotta get at him soon."

"Time will come soon," Parkman said quietly. "But you've got to be a little patient, an' we have to plan it."

Ben turned back to the horses, and for a moment Parkman thought he might still mount up and ride out to his death, but he just stood there. When he turned back to Parkman again, some of the tension had gone out of his face. He said, "You haven't pointed me wrong yet, an' maybe there is still one or two things you could teach me. Guess I'll play this one your way, too."

"Good," Parkman said. "Now the first thing is to find out a little more about how things stand around here. Only a fool bets his hand before he sees all his cards. Let's hang around town a few days an' listen to the talk, make a few friends if we can.

"An' we need to earn some money. There's only seven dollars and some coins in the poke. Evenings an' Sundays we'll ride around some. Check out the lay of the land. Might need to know that once we've made our play an' started out."

"Do you reckon we can afford to stable these horses an' get some oats in 'em?" Ben asked. "They're lookin' mighty lean."

"We'll have to afford it," Parkman said. "We'll need 'em strong an' spunky soon enough."

They started down the street, leading their two mounts toward the livery stable. The rancher Paulson came out of the saloon, and in a minute Ben realized that he was cutting across the street at an angle, headed the same place they were. By the time they reached the stable he was just a few feet behind them. At the door they paused and waited for him to come up to them.

"I been thinkin' about it," Paulson said without any preliminaries, "an' I've decided to offer you two boys a job. It's just ranch work, fifteen dollars a month an' board, but since you said your guns ain't for hire, you ain't gonna find much better around here."

Ben kept his mouth shut and let Ridge deal with the offer.

"It's mighty kind of you, Mr. Paulson," Ridge said, "but hirin' us wouldn't make you the most popular man in these parts. I don't really see why you'd want to."

"I just got a hunch I could trust you two," the rancher speculated. "It's gettin' harder to keep good hands. Salem's bunch keeps runnin' 'em off . . . but I have an idea you two wouldn't bluff like most."

"Sounds like you wouldn't mind us hirin' our guns out after all," Ridge said, "just so long as it's for your side."

"I ain't out lookin' for no gunslingers,"

Paulson said. "I got a lot of real honest to goodness cow punchin' that needs doin' on my spread, and them gun hands don't want to do nothin' but sit around on their duffs 'til it comes time to sling some lead. But I do like to hire men who will stay around an' can stay alive, too."

Parkman turned his head to his friend and said, "The job sound all right, Ben?"

"It sounds good," Ben said.

"Good, good," Paulson said. "Meet me over by the hardware store in half an hour. I've got some supplies to load, an' then I'll be ready to leave."

"Might as well start earnin' our pay right now," Ben said.

"Sure, we'll help you load," Parkman agreed.

CHAPTER SEVEN

Ben and Parkman tied their horses to the back of the wagon and rode on the seat beside Paulson. He was a rugged outdoorsman and a very talkative person. He looked the type of man who liked a laugh and a good time, the kind of man it was a pleasure to buy a drink for just to hear his banter, but he was not joking as he filled his two new hands in on the situation in the valley.

"We could always handle that younger Salem," he told them. "He spent more of his time runnin' that ranch than he did tryin' to run us out. But that brother of his is a different type of critter. I don't know how many men have died already. A sight of 'em disappeared, but we like to hope that most jus' yallered out and ran." The rancher spat a long stream of tobacco juice into the dust at the side of the road and then added, "Yep, boys, you've hired into a fine skillet of fish here."

"Seems like a man's not goin' to find a job nowhere where there ain't somethin' stirrin' these days," Parkman said. "The war's got everythin' all boggled up."

"We don't pay much attention to the war out here," Paulson said. "The news we get is weeks old, an' it's always bad anyway. A lot of folks dyin' back there, but there ain't but just a couple of our local boys got mixed up in it."

"There's been a plenty of killin'," Parkman agreed

"We got our own wars to fight out here, too. We're always fightin' somethin', draughts or Indians or rustlers or blackleg or skunks like them Salems. Then today in town I heard there's a bunch of roughnecks hidin' out in the mountains. Nobody knows who they're for. I figger they might be Salem's reserves, but he's not usin' 'em for anything. The man I talked to said they'd been up there a week or better, a dozen or more of 'em, and hadn't raised a hand 'gainst either side."

Ben did not say anything, but he knew he and Parkman were probably thinking the same thing. That was undoubtedly Firston and his bunch up there, biding their time while they figured out a way to get Salem and maybe make a dollar or two out of the mess in the valley to boot.

As the road started to climb gradually up the valley floor, Paulson checked his rifle and laid it across his lap. "We're gettin' close to Salem territory," he said. "Men die mysteriously around here. Rifle bullets come out of nowhere. You've gotta keep a sharp eye out. Some of that trash Salem's hired are sneaky as Indians."

Ben watched Parkman shift his revolver so it was a little easier to get at and then did the same. Of course if you were going to get it from behind a rock or bush, there was no way to stop it, but if the gunman missed the first time, it would be good to be able to throw a little lead back before a second shot could be fired.

The beauty of the valley belied the trouble that unscrupulous men had brought to it. The grazing land on both sides of the road stretched away, lush and rich, to the distant, jagged blue-gray beginnings of the mountains. Cattle were in sight most of the time, fat, healthy, prime animals. There was room and land here for many men who just wanted to make a comfortable living, but a greedy man like Salem, Ben knew, would see it as the perfect place for a beef empire.

Rubbing the moon-shaped scar on the back of his hand, which a boot heel had made in Salem's prison camp, Ben swore that Salem would never live long enough to enjoy any empire. Somewhere in this valley, right then, Salem was scheming and planning for the future, but he did not have much future left. His future was a bullet and a curse.

About halfway up the valley Paulson turned the wagon onto a smaller side road, which led toward a cluster of gentle green hills in the distance.

"My place is jus' outa sight up ahead, right smack on top of one of those hills," the rancher said. "I'm luckier than most. From my place I look down in all four directions, an' lately we've cleared away every tree an' rock an' bush big enough for a varmit to hide behind. If anybody decides to commence shootin' at us there, he's gonna have to be man enough to come out in the open to do it."

"Smart," Parkman commented. "Makes a lot of difference in a fight who's got the high ground."

The ranch buildings were all of simple rough-cut planks except for the ranch house. "When we come out here years ago," Paulson grinned, "My wife insisted on a white house. Wouldn't even let me build a barn first." In addition to the ranch house, there was a barn, cook shack, bunkhouse, and a few out-buildings and corrals.

At the house Paulson turned the reins over to Parkman and got down. "You boys take care of the team an' unload everything from the wagon. Foodstuffs go to the cook shack over there, an' the rest of the truck goes in the barn. Then get settled in the bunkhouse," he said. "You can meet the crew at supper tonight an' begin work at first light tomorrow morning."

As Parkman drove the wagon toward the barn, Ben asked, "What do you think?"

"Well," Parkman drawled, "it's three squares an' a bunk out of the rain."

"No, I mean about what's goin' on here in this valley."

"I think it's a wet camp downwind of a dead steer, but we knowed that 'fore we come here. Paulson didn't say that much we didn't already know."

"Except for the part about Firston."

"Yep. Guess we figgered the same when he told 'bout that bunch in the mountains. We're gonna have to give some thought to Firston. It's a good break that we got out of town so fast. If one of his men spotted us an' the word got out, we might have more than we could handle an' no friends on either side."

"I'm not goin' to lie low here very long, Ridge," Ben said. "I'm goin' after Salem as soon as I know where he is an' how to get there."

"You got time," Parkman advised. "One thing I learned in the war was not to charge 'til you know the lay of the land up ahead. Let's punch some steers or string some wire or whatever else Paulson has in mind for us. We'll learn a lot jus' listenin' to the talk of the men. You might find out some little something that'll keep you alive when you finally do go after Salem."

"I'll give it a while," Ben said. "But what I'd like to do is jus' ride over an' drop him an' to hell with what happened after."

"But if you got killed killin' him, what the hell kind of stupid revenge would that be? The best thing would be to get him an' make it out alive, too."

Ben had to admit the wisdom in what Parkman said.

They unloaded the wagon and fed and stabled the horses. As they were carrying their bedrolls and saddlebags toward the bunkhouse, six men, four on horseback and two in a wagon, rode up. Ben and Parkman went on to the bunkhouse, and a few minutes later the other cowboys came in. Both Ben and Parkman had put their gear on empty bunks at the far end of the row and were putting their few personal items on the shelves above their bunks.

Ben straightened up and turned when he heard a voice in the group at the other end of the room say, "Why, Curley, I believe that boy's takin' the bunk you decided to move to. Reckon who he is to be so uppity?"

"I don't know," the one called Curley answered, "but I'm sure he an' I can talk it over an' get it straight. He looks like a boy that don't want no trouble."

Slowly, but obviously, Parkman turned and began unbuckling his gun belt. "It's a cowboy bunkhouse game, Ben," he explained loudly enough that the cowboys could hear. "They've gotta see if we got grit in our gullets, an' we've gotta crack a few heads to prove we're tough enough to deserve the pleasure of their company. Won't take us a minute, an' then we can get on with this unpackin'."

He turned to the group of surprised men and said, "How do you gents prefer to fight? Regular or Injun-style?" Nobody answered. "They look like fair fighters, Ben," Parkman continued. "So don't bite off no ears nor poke no eyes out."

The cowboys were standing in a group, canteens and saddlebags still in hand, wondering what kind of crazy men they had bothered.

"See, I have to remind my friend here," Parkman said quietly but convincingly. "We jus' come from a place where nobody bothered to fight for fun. When we went at a man, somebody died. It's been a while since either of us fought for fun, but let's go outside an' get it over with. I'm hungry."

The group stood quietly for a moment, but finally one big, red-faced cowboy stepped forward and, with a wide, friendly grin, extended his hand and said, "I'll take you for a pardner in any card game. You've got one of the best bluffs I ever seen. They call me Curley."

What followed happened so fast that nobody realized what was going on until it was over. With one hand Ridge snatched the pistol from Curley's holster and with the other he doubled him up with a punch square into his breadbasket. "A man don't bluff on a pat hand," Parkman drawled amiably. "An' I've already got a pardner."

Curley sat back abruptly on one of the bunks and began to laugh as he caught his wind. "I can see you an' me is goin' to be goin' round an' round for some time," he said, his chuckles interspersed with grunts and coughs. The other men joined in the laughter and began to step forward to shake Ben and Parkman's hands.

The food that the old whiskered cook served was simple but good. After months of eating their own rough cooking on the trail, Ben and Parkman ate the thick beef stew and cornbread until the other men began to make jokes about hollow legs and eating up all the boss's profits.

After supper the cowboys, one by one, wandered out of the cook shack, carrying tin cups of coffee, to sit on the steps of the bunkhouse and build cigarettes while they talked over the day's work.

The two new men joined them, but they did little to join in the talk. They listened, trying to learn something about the men they would be working with. It was all new to Ben. He knew little about a cowboy's life and work. The most cows he and his father had ever owned was twelve, and they had required little tending.

Still he felt a sort of warm kinship with these men. They were rough and burly, and their talk was crude, drifting from cow punching to women and drinking, but they were friendly and open to the two new men who had joined them, and Ben appreciated that. He had already, after only a few hours of being around them, come to feel a part of this group, and he was proud of it.

Near dark Paulson came over to the bunkhouse, and he and Curley, who was evidently a sort of foreman, discussed what work would be done the next day. It was decided that Ben, who was inexperienced, would go on the fencing crew, and Ridge would ride with the rest of the cowboys to herd back some stray cattle that had been seen in a ravine back toward the mountains.

The talk grew serious when they began to discuss the mountains in back of the ranch. That was where the unidentified band of men had been seen, and Paulson cautioned his men to keep one hand on their rifles at all times and not to stray too far from one another.

"Cowhands are hard to find these days," Paulson said. "I'd be hard put to replace any of you men if you got yourself shot up."

"We wouldn't be too fond of havin' to be replaced that way either," one of the cowboys quipped. He was a weathered beanpole of a man with lively, humorous eyes. The others called him Rex.

"I'm sure that's true enough," Paulson chuckled. He turned to Ben and Ridge and asked, "You two men gettin' on okay?"

"Shore are," Ridge drawled. "We all hit it

off right away."

"Glad to hear it," Paulson said. "Sometimes a new man has a hard time gettin' settled in with this bunch of rowdies. I've heard some strange noises come from that bunkhouse once in a while." He grinned knowingly as he glanced around the group of cowboys. It was easy to see that he was proud of his rough-and-tumble crew. "Funny thing, though," he added innocently. "I never seem to get out there in time to find out what was goin' on."

"We jus' fall down once in a while, Mr. Paulson," Rex laughed. "There ain't a spoonful of grace in the whole lot of us."

They turned in early that evening, which suited Ben fine. It had been a long, eventful day.

CHAPTER EIGHT

Ben woke to the sounds of men stirring around, yawning and grumbling as they pulled on jeans and boots. At the opposite end of the room, Curley, in long johns and socks, was lighting a kerosene lamp. Sitting on the bunk next to Ben, Ridge was almost dressed already. "These folks get up before the roosters," he grinned as he reached for his boots.

Ridge plunged one foot down in his boot, then quickly let out a curse and jerked his foot out again.

"What the . . . ?" he mumbled as he looked in the boot. The ripe smell of fresh manure reached Ben's nostrils about the same time Ridge began a string of oaths at nobody in particular.

"What is it, pard?" Rex asked with concern, barely disguising the humor on his face.

"Reckon what kind of rotten hombre

would do that to a man?" asked another cowboy named Vegas.

"Might be Mrs. Paulson's milk cow's been walkin' in her sleep again," a third cowboy suggested. "That's a real problem critter. Strolls around at night, droppin' piles in the damndest places."

Down at the other end of the room Curley was taking an unusually long time to get the lamp adjusted.

Ben just couldn't help but laugh as he watched Ridge pull off his sticky, smelly sock. "Go ahead an' laugh," Ridge said good-naturedly. "I bet you stop laughin' real sudden like in a minute though when you go to put your boots on."

Ben snatched up his boots and examined them. The left one was heavy with a smelly load. He dressed and then went out with Parkman to wash the boot out at the pump in the yard. When they had finished they joined the other men at the cook shack. The incident was not mentioned again, but all through breakfast Ben and Ridge caught some of the others glancing at them occasionally and chuckling. But both of them took it good-naturedly because they knew that, besides being a humorous prank, it was also a test to see how well they were going to get along.

The breakfast was as good and plentiful as supper had been. Ben could not help but think back to his prison days, when the same amount of food he got here would have been divided up among four or five prisoners. Rex, who Ben was to help on the fencing, told Ben that they would be working near enough that they could come back for lunch. The cook wrapped bundles of meat and biscuits in cloth for the other men.

After breakfast Ben went to the barn and loaded barbed wire on the wagon as Rex harnessed the horses. While they were working, the other men saddled up and left.

" 'Fore we leave, you'd best go up to the house and get a rifle from the boss, son," Rex said. "That six-shooter's all right for close-up fightin', but out on the range a rifle's the thing."

"I like a rifle better anyway," Ben told him.

"Mr. Paulson's got some beauties. He'll let you use one."

After saddling his horse and tying it on the back of the wagon as Rex had done, Ben went to the house for the gun. He went to the back door because he had learned that was the door most of the men approached the main house from. The Paulsons were just finishing breakfast. Ben's first impression of the boss's wife was a good one. She was middle-aged and plain, as he had expected, but her good nature and friendliness made Ben feel comfortable and welcome.

" 'Scuse me," he said. "But Rex said I might, could borrow a rifle from you."

"Good idea," Paulson said, rising from his chair. "I meant to say something about it yesterday. I saw you didn't have one." He left the room.

"I guess you've eaten already, but would you like some coffee?" Mrs. Paulson offered. "You're one of the men my husband hired in town yesterday, aren't you?"

"Yes, ma'am, I am," Ben said. "I appreciate the invite, but I guess I better get out an' start earnin' my keep. Rex is waitin' to go."

"Well, feel free to come up any time. If you need any buttons sewed or holes patched, let me know. Men are all thumbs and elbows with a needle and thread."

"Thank you, ma'am."

Paulson came back in a moment with the rifle. "Is this Henry 44 all right?" he asked.

"Fine," Ben said. "It'll feel good to hold a rifle in my hands again. Makes a man feel safer."

"That's 'specially true 'round these parts," Paulson said bitterly.

"It's just awful," Mrs. Paulson said sadly. "Things used to be so peaceful here in the valley."

"Well, maybe things will work themselves out," Ben said.

"We'll work them out soon enough," Paulson said.

"Now Adrian . . ." Mrs. Paulson said.

"Thanks for the loan," Ben said, taking the rifle and a box of cartridges from his boss.

Rex was waiting out front with the wagon. Ben got up on the seat beside him and they left. The stretch of fence they were to work on was a couple of miles from the house. As Rex drove the wagon along the line of posts, Ben was in back dropping off the rolls of wire.

Rex kept up a running dialogue about matters of the valley. He talked about how it had been before the Salems came in and began buying up land, and about the discouraging changes that had gone on since.

After all the wire was dropped off, they went back and started putting it up. It was hard work in the blazing sun, but Ben was amazed at how he stood up to it. Back in his prison days he would have dropped from exhaustion before the morning was half over, but that was when he had existed on small amounts of food and received almost daily beatings. His strength and fitness had increased rapidly since he had escaped and he had regained almost all of the good health he always had before entering the prison camp.

Rex decided from the sun when it was noon and time to head back for lunch. They hobbled the wagon team and mounted to ride back on the saddle horses.

Just as they were turning to ride away, a shot rang out some distance away and out of sight behind a nearby hill.

Ben and Rex both grabbed their rifles and leaped to the ground. They could not tell what was happening for a minute. Other shots sounded, but they were all too far away to be aimed at the two men. They stood behind the wagon and waited.

Then a lone horse and rider came tearing from behind the hill, running wide open. The horse went at a right angle to them for a while, but then the rider seemed to spot the wagon and headed for it. A few seconds later two more horses came in sight, hotly pursuing the first. They were firing with their rifles at the first rider.

As the single rider got closer, Rex said, "Well I'll be dead and buried! That's Miss Clarice!" Ben recognized the name immediately as the girl who had helped him and Parkman out of jail the day before. Both of them drew beads on the riders in pursuit, but they were still too far away to shoot at.

"Just a little closer an' it'll be worth takin' a crack at 'em," Rex said, sighting down the worn barrel of his rifle. But the riders seemed to know that and pulled up. "Damn!" Rex muttered.

But Ben was still aiming. As the riders stopped for a more careful aim at the girl, Ben squeezed off a shot. A couple of seconds passed when the world seemed frozen except for the figure of horse and girl dashing across the flatland. Then one of the distant riders toppled off his horse and lay still on the ground. The other rider pranced his horse around, undecided for a moment, then turned and rode away at full gallop.

"Hot damn, what a shot!" Rex said in wonder. He turned to Ben and slapped him hard on the back. "I ain't never seen no shootin' like that. You knocked that feller slap outa the saddle."

"I aimed four foot over his head," Ben grinned. "It was jus' luck."

"All I know is what I saw," Rex insisted, "an' I saw you lay that hombre low."

In a moment the girl reached them. She half-stepped down, half-dropped into Rex's arms. "I don't know your name, cowboy," she said to Rex breathlessly, "But if you'll tell me, I'll never forget it."

"Name's Rex, ma'am," Rex said, "but you owe your thanks to Ben here. Never saw such shootin' as he jus' done."

Clarice turned to Ben and immediately recognized him. "The bank robber," she laughed. "I'm sure glad now that I helped you get out of jail."

"I'm glad, too," Ben said. "But that shot was jus' the purest luck. Maybe you've got an angel lookin' out for you."

"Might be, but I'll settle for a crack shot like you looking out for me any day."

Ben was so flustered by the compliment that he could not answer. Rex laughed and slapped Ben's back again.

Ben turned and busied himself unhobbling the wagon horses. "We'll have to go pick that man up," he said. "You or somebody back at the ranch might know who he is."

"All right, Ben," Rex said. "I'll handle the team and you cover." He turned to Clarice and told her, "Wait here for us, miss. We'll be back in a minute."

They rode out to where the body lay. Ben kept a close watch on the hill behind which the second rider had fled, though he knew the man was probably far away by then. The dead man lay on his stomach in a crumpled heap. There was a gaping wound in his back where the bullet had ripped out. As Ben watched, Rex jumped down and rolled the body over.

Ben did not think he knew the dead man, but his face was covered with a heavy beard and layers of dirt so it was impossible to be certain. Ben had only been around Firston's men for one day several weeks ago, so he was not sure whether the dead man could have been a member of that gang or not. He did not remember the faces of all the men.

Rex leaned down and inspected the face closely. "Nope," he finally decided. "I don't know the gent." Together they loaded the body on the wagon and covered it with a piece of canvas.

When they got back to where they had been working, Rex decided that they should load up the tools and take them in. They would have to go into town and tell the sheriff what had happened so they would not get back to work that day.

Clarice said she would ride her horse to the ranch house instead of riding the wagon. It surprised Ben how quickly she snapped back to normal after just having her life threatened and seeing a man killed. The West, he decided, bred hardier women. She was definitely not the kind of girl he was used to seeing back where he was raised.

She and Ben rode together a short distance behind the wagon, and it made him nervous to be so near her. It had been a long time since he had had any companion except other men. He thought back to the days at home before the war, to the fading memories of his boyhood, of going to church sociables, walking hand in hand down the road with some girl and stealing a kiss behind the wagon as their parents loaded up to go home. It was another world, a dead world. The farms had become scarred battlefields, the churches made into headquarters or field hospitals or put to the torch so the enemy could not use them.

"I'm really grateful, Ben," Clarice said with a pleasant smile. Her voice brought him back to the present. "My horse was about worn out, and they would have caught me soon . . . but doesn't it make you feel strange to kill a man like that, so suddenly I mean? Didn't you hesitate just a second before you were finally able to pull the trigger?"

"Some other time I might have," Ben told her. "But jus' then I didn't have time to think about it. He had drawn down on you, an' in another second it would have been too late. I jus' shot as soon as I saw him stop."

A slight shift of the wind brought a whiff of her sweet perfume to him. He turned his head just to take in her prettiness. She was looking forward, but she seemed to feel his eyes on her because she turned to meet his gaze and smiled again. Irrationally he felt a sudden hunger just to reach out and touch her. That one momentary look she gave him filled an emptiness in him that he never knew existed before.

But the moment was brief. Rex spit out a long stream of tobacco juice and called back, "You want to go on in to the ranch with us, Miss Clarice, or ride back to your daddy's place? The turnoff is just up ahead, and I don't figger Ben would object too strong to escourtin' you home."

"I think I'll go home," Clarice said, "that is, if Ben doesn't mind the imposition."

"Beats stringin' wire, don't it, Ben?" Rex said sarcastically.

"It beats a lot of things, I guess," Ben said.

As they parted company at the turnoff, Rex told Ben, "After Miss Clarice is home safe, ride on into town an' wait for me. I'll go by the ranch an' tell the boss, an' then

I'll haul this owlhoot into town. I figger we'd best get him in today or he'll get ripe on us."

"Sure, Rex," Ben said. "I'll wait for you in town."

It was pure enjoyment for Ben to ride alongside the attractive girl, to hear the music of her laughter, and watch her long, auburn hair blow in the wind. After his first shyness had faded, he also found her interesting and easy to talk to.

"I guess my days of riding alone are over," she said. "Papa had warned me before about it; but I never took him seriously until today.

"All my life it has been so peaceful around here that I guess I thought it would never be any different. When I was a girl, I was wild as an Indian. I used to go off for days at a time, riding these hills and mountains. I knew every cave and rock and bobcat den up there.

"I had to learn to like being alone when I was a girl. There weren't very many children to play with. Maybe once a week one of the neighbors would come by or we'd go visiting and I'd have other children to play with, but I guess it's okay to grow up that way. You learn to be more independent, to rely on yourself and be happy with your own company . . . I guess I'll have a lot of adjusting to do when I marry Joe."

Ben had nearly forgotten about the banker's son and about Clarice's engagement to him. Although he knew it was ridiculous, he was jealous and found himself wishing he knew something bad to say about Joe. But he reminded himself that he was just taking her home and would probably never have the chance to be around her again. He kept his silence.

"I guess I know what you think about Joe after the way he acted in town yesterday," Clarice said, "but usually he does not act so terribly. He just gets excited, and he lets his mouth get away from him. I'm very fond of him."

That seemed to Ben a strange way for a girl to talk about the man she planned to marry. It was as if she were explaining away the faults of some naughty child rather than talking about her future husband. And it seemed to him that she should be more than just fond of him.

"I don't know him, except what I saw of him yesterday in town," Ben said. "If he stays out of my hair I won't be thinkin' no more 'bout him one way or the other."

It was a thirty-minute ride to Broken Cross, the ranch belonging to Clarice's father, Harvey Morgan. The ranch house and grounds were similar to Paulson's spread. Ben and Clarice rode up to the ranch house, and she invited him to dismount and go in with her. "You'll have plenty of time to meet your friend in town," she said. "In that wagon it'll take him much longer. I'm sure my mother and father will want to thank you."

"Maybe I'd better just stay out on the porch," Ben suggested. "I'm too dirty to spend much time in polite company."

"This is cattle country, Ben. We all get dirty here, and we're used to it."

Clarice led him through the hallway and into what seemed to be the ranch office. The two men seated in the room rose as Clarice came in. The one that the girl went to and kissed, Ben knew, must be her father. The other man in the room was Joe Guthrie, Clarice's fiancé.

"What in the world are you doing riding up with a cowboy?" Joe demanded before anyone else could speak. After glaring a moment at Clarice, he looked more closely at Ben and exclaimed, "Isn't he one of those men we put in jail yesterday?"

"Ben was escorting me home. . . ." Clarice began.

"You can't just go riding around the country with any saddle scruff you run into," Joe said hotly. "And then to bring him home with you . . . there's no telling what people will start saying about you . . . and me!"

Ben had not been too pleased to see Guthrie in the first place, but the name calling was too much for him to take. He took a couple of threatening steps forward and said, "If you're goin' to throw that kind of talk at a man, you're goin' to have to face up to what comes after."

It surprised and unnerved the young man to be answered so suddenly. He began fumbling at the buttons of his jacket, but it appeared that he would rather find some fast way out of the room than to try to get to his gun.

"Wait a minute, Ben," Clarice said. Ben glanced at her and was pleased to see her eyes flashing angrily as she advanced on her fiancé. "This man just saved my life, Joe Guthrie! I won't abide another rude word from you. Either you keep quiet or leave this minute!"

"What happened, honey?" Morgan asked.

"Some men were chasing me and shooting at me," the girl said. "Ben shot one of them and scared the other one off. I would be dead now if it weren't for him."

Morgan came to Ben and shook his hand

enthusiastically. "We're obliged to you, cowboy. This girl means quite a bit to her mother an' me."

"She's worth fightin' for," Ben blurted out, and then was embarrassed at his own words.

"I'm glad you think so," Clarice laughed. "Where would I be if you didn't think I was worth the price of a bullet?"

Ben and her father laughed, but Guthrie remained in the background glowering.

"It was jus' repayin' a favor anyway," Ben said. "Some fellas in town yesterday had me an' my friend sized up as bank robbers, and your daughter got us off the hook."

"She told us about it," Morgan said, casting a significant glance back at Guthrie.

"It was a pretty bad way to start 'round here," Ben said, "but things have been goin' fine since. We got a job with Mr. Paulson the same day."

"Well, if Adrian Paulson trusts you, that's recommendation enough for any man," Morgan said. "Clarice, take Ben in the parlor an' find him a seat while I go get your mother."

Against Ben's objections about his dirty clothes, Clarice led him into another room, and they settled into overstuffed chairs. Guthrie followed dourly. He stood in the doorway sulking until Clarice said, "For heaven's sake, Joe, sit down!" He took a seat across the room from Ben.

The silence in the room was awkward until Morgan returned with his wife. She was a small, attractive woman of about fifty. Ben could tell from her aging beauty where Clarice had inherited her dazzling good looks.

Mrs. Morgan was almost in tears when she said, "We're so grateful, young man." Ben rose and was startled when she kissed him on the cheek. "I've told her not to ride alone and so has her father, but she sneaks off, and she's too big to spank. I guess she'll know better now."

"I will, mama," Clarice said quietly.

"Any idea who the men were?" Morgan asked.

"Rex said he didn't know the one I shot," Ben said. "We didn't get a look at the other one."

"Makes a man mad," Morgan said bitterly, "havin' the kind of scum around who would bother defenseless women. Pretty soon when folks get mad enough in this valley . . ."

"We're all afraid of what's going to happen soon," Mrs. Morgan said seriously.

Clarice's mother served coffee, and the

five of them sat and talked for a few minutes. Clarice told her parents what had happened, and Ben was amused to see the story already begin to grow and take on embellishments. He sat quietly and did not contradict her as she exaggerated about the rifle shot that had brought down her assailant. As the talk went on to other subjects, Ben could tell that they were curious and would like for him to volunteer some personal information about himself, but he made no mention of his own background or the circumstances that had brought him to the valley. It was quite a while before Ben remembered that he had to meet Rex in town.

The whole family walked him to the door. As he was standing on the porch saying his farewells, Clarice came near to him and said, "I guess I owe you as much thanks as my mother." The kiss she placed on his stubbled cheek sent chills through him.

"I . . . uh . . . thanks . . ." he stammered.

Mrs. Morgan and her husband laughed at his awkwardness. "You've embarrassed him," she chided her daughter gently.

"It's been a while since I got a kiss," Ben admitted, "an' kisses from two pretty ladies in one day is a little bit much for me to handle."

"Well, you'll get one every time you save my life," Clarice said lightly.

"I reckon that's enough to make a man keep a sharp eye out," Ben said as he mounted his horse.

As he rode away he scarcely knew what to think about the events of the past few hours. But on the ride to town his happiness settled slowly into a quiet depression. It was just a fluke to get attention from a girl like Clarice. Her life was settled, and soon she would forget. There was no common ground between them where they could ever meet again. She would go on to marry a banker's son and live in a pretty house in town, and as for Ben, he had himself a man to kill.

A storm was building over the mountains behind Ben as he neared town. He glanced back occasionally to watch the heavy thunderclouds roll up to follow him toward town. The first raindrops began falling as he rode into town. As he rode down the wide, main street, he watched the puffs of dust rise as the raindrops struck the road.

He spotted the wagon Rex was driving down the street and rode to it. It was stopped in front of a building that had a sign on the front reading "Carpenter." Ben dismounted and tied his horse to the back of the wagon. There were several men crowded around the room. The body of the man he shot was lying on the workbench in the middle of the room. Ben spotted Rex on one side of the table talking to the sheriff and went over to him.

"Anybody know who he is?" he asked Rex.

"None of these fellers do," Rex said, "and I guess among 'em they know about everybody hereabouts."

"He could be one of Salem's new guns," the sheriff said. "That's who we figure he's got to be . . . unless he's part of that bunch up in the mountains."

Ben took a close look again at the dead man. He still did not recognize him, but he was trying to memorize his features so he could describe the man to Ridge later.

The corpse had a mean, sharp-featured face. Partly concealed under his beard was an ugly, badly healed scar, which ran from beneath his left ear down across his face to his chin. It was a ragged-edged furrow, which Ben thought was probably made by a bullet.

It would be impossible to guess the dead man's age. He was probably between thirty and forty, but he could have been a younger man with features prematurely aged by hard living and layers of dirt. He had a lean, muscular body, but with the slight paunch of a heavy drinker. One leg seemed to be slightly shorter than the other.

"You get that coffin built an' get him planted," the sheriff told one of the men in the room. "I'll get the town to pay you for it."

"I'll get it done, sheriff," the man answered. He was a short, husky man with calloused, strong-looking hands. He was easily identified as the carpenter by the traces of sawdust that clung to his face and arms. "I'll get him in the ground, but it won't be nothin' fancy. I always put his type facedown. Let 'em see where they're goin'."

The other men chuckled, but the carpenter appeared to be serious about what he said.

"Let's go to the office an' talk," the sheriff said to Rex and Ben. "I want to hear this story straight through so there's no question about what happened."

"Anything you say, Sy," Rex said.

"I don't think anything'll come of it," the sheriff said, "but somebody might come in later an' say you two ambushed them an' killed this man."

They spent nearly a half hour with the sheriff telling him the events of the day. When they came out it was nearly dark, and the rain had settled into a steady downpour.

"I could use a glass of whiskey," Rex said. "This ain't exactly been what you'd call your average work day."

"I'm right with you," Ben said.

As they neared the saloon Ben glanced across the street and noticed Joe Guthrie coming out of the bank building. "You go ahead," he told Rex. "I'll be along in a minute."

Rex seemed to sense that something was about to happen. As Ben started away he stepped back into a doorway to wait and watch. Ben sloshed through the muddy street and caught up with Guthrie. He caught him by the arm and turned him around roughly.

"Now you keep your mouth shut an' listen," Ben ordered. "I ain't goin' to beat the cussedness out of you right now, 'cause if I got started I'm not sure I could get stopped. But I want to let you know if I ever have to tie into you, I'll turn you every way but loose. You're goin' to have to learn that you have to back up what comes out of your mouth with your fists an' your gun, or else life is goin' to be real hard an' real short for you."

Guthrie sputtered in surprise and started to say something, but Ben gave him a hard shove backward into the street, and he fell splattering into the mud.

Rex was chuckling when Ben got back to him. As they started walking again, Rex said, "You want to say what that was all about?"

"A little disagreement," Ben said as he pushed open the saloon doors and went in. Over drinks he told Rex about his visit to the Morgan house and about the way Guthrie had acted. He left out the part about Clarice's kiss. He knew it would only mean endless ragging from the crew, and he thought he would have to fight if much of that went on.

Rather than ride back in the rain, they bunked that night on the clean hay in the livery stable and rode back to the ranch at dawn.

CHAPTER NINE

The days passed quickly as Ben and Ridge settled into the work routine of the ranch. Ben dedicated himself to learning the countless jobs that had to be done to keep a ranch going. He worked mostly with Rex, fencing, mending corrals and equipment, and doctoring sick animals. Occasionally he was allowed to ride with the crew and quickly picked up the techniques of cowboying.

For the first couple of weeks he never left the ranch. Ridge rode once into town with the other hands on Saturday night. As Ben watched them leave, he wondered why they went in the wagon instead of on horseback, but when he heard them return and went out to meet them, he found his answer. Only one or two of them was sober enough to even have a chance of staying in the saddle. Ridge and Curley were both passed out and lay in the back of the wagon like corpses.

Few of the others showed many signs of life.

The next morning in daylight, Ben saw that Curley's face was swollen and covered with plum-colored bruises. Ridge's condition was almost as bad, and he told Ben later that he and Curley had settled the question of whether a man should fill another man's boot with cow dung.

Ben and Rex were the only ones to show up at the cook shack for breakfast. The rest struggled to life one by one all morning. In midafternoon Ben noticed Mr. Paulson come out of the house and take a chair on the front porch. Ben strolled over and took a seat on the porch step.

"I saw Harvey Morgan in town this morning at church," Paulson said. "We were talking about you, an' he said you had some disagreement with young Guthrie a week or two ago."

Ben grinned and said, "He's not easy to get along with, an' we got off on the wrong foot right at the start. I guess we agreed the other day we'd just as soon stay away from one another."

"Might be the best thing from what I hear," Paulson agreed. "That boy might have the brains, but he's mighty short on horse sense." He paused for a moment, shifting slightly in his chair, and then added offhandedly, "Clarice asked 'bout how you were doin', too."

That caught Ben off guard. He avoided Paulson's eyes when he said, "There's another dead end."

Paulson did not comment, but in a moment Ben found himself opening up to the older man. "I can't see no future in moonin' over any real lady. I guess you've figured out by now that me an' Ridge came here from the war." The older man nodded. "Well, that does somethin' to a man. It eats his heart out. I ain't aimin' to give myself any hurts with wild dreams about Clarice. I just figger to get by with three squares an' a couple of dollars in my pocket 'til I find some sense in life again."

"A man don't know what he can do or get 'til he tries," Paulson said. "I come out here with nothin', an' I ain't sayin' I got all that much now, but this place ain't that bad. An' I'm jus' an average man."

"It's a fine place," Ben said. He was anxious to get the talk going in another direction. A moment before when he had been talking, it felt good to tell his feelings to someone, but immediately afterward he felt vulnerable about opening up. It was the old prison conditioning, he knew. The best policy had always been to keep your mouth shut and never let it be seen that anything happening to you or going on around you had any effect on you.

Since his visit to the Morgan ranch he had been fighting any thoughts about the girl. He was convinced it was the only smart thing to do. Casually, he hoped, he asked if the Salems came into town to church.

"Their women come," Paulson said. "It's really women that keep the churches goin' out here. Only reason I go is my wife makes it hard on me if I don't. But it's good. Reminds me once in a while I owe a debt."

"I guess," Ben said. "I don't think on that stuff much."

"Jude Salem used to come to church before his brother come out here. I used to know him some, but now he an' his brother stay holed up. They send their women down to town with a crew of six or eight outriders."

"Must be hard on the women."

"I reckon, but it's a man's world out here," Paulson said. "When I look back on how it's been, I can mostly remember fightin'. An' that's man's work. The most part women have in it is that they're what we usually are fightin' for. To make a good life for them."

"Is Salem goin' to win out?" Ben asked.

"Since I been here, all I hear is how he's gettin' together an army."

"He might," Paulson said sadly. "But it'll be 'cause he's buried us, not 'cause he run us out."

Ben admired the old man's spirit. He thought he could fight again for a man like this. It was so different from the war, where a man fought and killed and died because of orders and not because of beliefs.

Paulson took out his pipe and stuffed it full of tobacco, then passed the tobacco bag and a package of papers to Ben. As Ben began to build a cigarette, Paulson said tiredly, "I just wish it could always be like this. When we finished with the Indians, we thought . . . well, I'm jus' gettin' old an' tired. I turned fifty-two last month. Jus' seems like things could be quiet these last few years." Paulson's eyes drifted out over the range and seemed to fix on some point far away. He had forgotten to light his pipe. Ben shifted uncomfortably on the step.

After a few moments Paulson said, "It's Sunday, an' a man's s'posed to be thoughtful on Sunday . . . but action is all that counts for anything in this valley."

The next week was spent mostly in the ravines and small passes between the ranch and the mountains rounding up strays. The hands had found the carcasses of several steers with part of the meat gone, and Paulson was beginning to suspect that the mysterious band of men in the mountains was living off his cows. His men were spending most of their time herding the cattle nearer to the ranch where it would be easier to hear a shot and watch the herd.

Each time Ben rode out with the cowboys he learned more about what he was supposed to do and felt less like a hindrance to the rest of the crew. He reluctantly, swallowed a lot of good-natured kidding about being a greenhorn and a dude. Occasionally his temper flared, but he began to control it when he realized that making him flare up was one of the greatest pleasures to the men who kidded him.

Even Ridge indulged in some of the banter when they were in a group, but alone they did not waste time on it. They talked of Firston's men in the mountains and Salem's in the valley.

Saturday afternoon the men returned to the ranch early on Curley's instructions. After stabling their horses, they all went to the front of the ranch house. In a few minutes Paulson came out and began paying them their monthly wages.

The men were all in a gay mood, and Ben and Ridge felt as happy as the rest. The fifteen dollars Paulson gave Ben was the most money he had ever had at one time in his life. He had not actually even thought about getting the money until that day, and he had no idea what he wanted to do with it.

As they walked back to the bunkhouse, the other men were in an active discussion of the ways they were going to enjoy their wages. Even Rex seemed to be planning to go to town that night for a few drinks.

In the bunkhouse, razors, mirrors, soap, towels, and clean clothes were hauled out, and the men began to make themselves presentable.

Ben heard some of the other men discussing a dance, which was to be held in town that evening, and soon after he decided that it was time for him to get away from the ranch for a while. Of course, he told himself, it had nothing to do with Clarice. She probably would not be there, and even if she was, well, he was just going in for a few drinks with the boys.

Ben took his turn washing up in the horse trough. It felt good to scrub a week's dirt and stink off. It was something he seldom had the chance to do in the last few years.

He could still remember the stench of filthy bodies crowded close together on the plank floors of the prison. It was something he had never gotten used to, and he knew he would never forget it.

Late in the afternoon Ben saddled his and Ridge's horses and tied them to the back of the wagon. They had agreed earlier that they might want to come back early from town and would not want to wait for the rest of the men.

Ben piled in the rear of the wagon with the rest of the crew, and Rex clicked the horses into action. On the advice of Ridge he had left part of his money behind with Mrs. Paulson. His friend had done the same after telling him of slickers who skillfully lured just-paid cowhands into card games and sent them home broke. Ben was ashamed to tell Ridge that he did not know how to play poker, so he just left the money without saying anything.

The men laughed and joked and sang on the ride to town. One suggested a shooting contest, but Rex and Curley quickly vetoed the idea. Shots might bring unwanted visitors, or they might bring friends out on a useless ride.

Trinity Wells was busier than Ben had seen it before. The board sidewalks were lined with strolling men, and the hitching racks in front of the four saloons were crowded with tied horses. Rex let the men out in the center of town and drove the wagon down the street to the livery stable.

Ben followed along with the group. Curley and Vegas were in the lead, and Ben and Parkman brought up the rear. At the doorway to the first saloon, Ben paused. "What's the matter?" Ridge asked. "Not in a drinkin' mood?"

"I don't know," Ben said. "I wouldn't mind a couple of drinks, but I got to thinkin' on the way in about boots and maybe a new shirt. Do you think I got enough to buy them? Maybe I could save up a couple of months if I don't."

Ridge laughed out loud. "You've got plenty. Them things won't cost but three or four dollars."

"Well I guess I'll go and buy them first so I'm sure to have enough money."

Ridge looked reluctantly inside the saloon and then back at Ben. "All right. I guess I can wait a while to start. I'll stroll over with you."

Inside the general store Ben felt wealthy as he surveyed the line of boxed boots and stacks of new clothes. There were many types of boots, and impulsively Ben almost bought a soft, tooled-leather pair, but then he got to thinking about working in such dazzling footwear and decided that a more conventional pair would be more practical and comfortable. He also bought a bright, red plaid shirt and new pants and changed into his purchases in the back room of the store.

When Ben came back out in the front of the store, Ridge surveyed him and said, "That oughta make the ladies sit up an' pay attention."

"That wasn't really why I bought 'em," Ben said. "Those old duds I got from Firston were 'bout gone, an' these ones Rex loaned me to wear into town are 'bout as bad." As they left the store Ben stashed his old boots and shirt under the sidewalk, planning to come back for them later.

Walking down the sidewalk Ben felt odd and a little uncomfortable in the new clothes and boots. The last new clothing he had worn was the uniform the Confederate army had given him when they took him in. Even the prison uniform he had been given was old and frayed, taken off a recently dead prisoner and given to him still wet and steaming from the kettle of water where it had been boiled to kill the lice.

The rest of the ranch hands were gathered

around a big, round table in one of the saloons and had finished off half a bottle of whiskey by the time Ben and Parkman joined them. Their spirits were high, and everybody was trying to buy drinks for everybody else.

The whole saloon was crowded with other cowboys doing the same thing. All of the tables in the room were filled, and the long, mahogany bar was crowded with men standing shoulder to shoulder trying to get the bartender's attention. The room rocked with laughter and loud, masculine talk.

Some of Paulson's men were talking about going to the dance, and others were planning a visit to the "fancy house." Ben was not exactly sure what sort of house that might be, but he did not ask anybody about it. He was getting tired of being the ignorant kid, and he hoped he could have a night off from the kidding.

Ben was sitting with his back to the main part of the room so he did not see what happened to start the excitement. The first he knew that trouble was starting was when a man came hurtling backward by him and crashed into the wall. The big, husky cowboy stood leaning against the wall for a moment, a stupid grin on his face. He wiped his mouth with the back of his hand, glancing down at the blot of blood he had wiped off, and then hurled himself at his assailant. In a moment the saloon was swallowed up in chaos.

"Damn," Ridge muttered. "It always seems to happen. Cowboys can't seem to enjoy themselves unless they're poundin' on one another."

"I'd as soon stay out of it," Ben said.

"Me too," Ridge said. "My bones ached for a week after that scuffle with Curley. Let's get out of here." Making it to the front door was out of the question, so Ben and Ridge pushed their way through the crowd and left by the back door.

The cool evening air felt good to Ben. The saloon had been hot and smoky, and the two whiskeys he had slugged down had gone straight to his head. No one had eaten supper before leaving the ranch, and Ben was not accustomed to whiskey. His only acquaintance with liquor had been a few boyish bouts with the white lightning that the hill men made back home, and those had usually left him sick and hung over for days.

They walked behind the building and started up an alley, but just as they were about to emerge onto the main street, Ridge gripped Ben's arm and said, "Wait." He

pointed across the street to two men loung-
ing in front of a store, and said, "I recognize
those two. They're some of Firston's men."

They started to back into the shadows
against one wall of a building, but the two
men had already spotted them. One pointed
across at them and made some comment to
the other. Both shifted slightly on their seats
so that their guns were more available. "I
guess they recognize me," Ridge said. "You
wait here while I go over and parley for a
minute." He stepped out of the shadows
and started across the street toward them.

Both men rose to their feet when they saw
Ridge coming. Beneath theirs and Ridge's
casualness, Ben could sense the tenseness.
Everybody's hands hung freely within inches
of their guns.

Ridge walked directly up to them, and
both grudgingly shook his hand when he
extended it to them. Ben could hear their
voices, but he was not able to make out
what they were saying. After talking for a
moment, the three of them turned and
began walking away toward the deserted
end of town.

Ben could not decide whether to try and
follow along in the shadows in case Ridge
needed help, or to stay where he was and
wait for his friend. After they had gone

several yards and had their backs turned, he stepped out of the shadows onto the sidewalk.

A movement down the sidewalk caught Ben's eye, and he turned his head to see who it was. In a moment he spotted what had attracted his attention. It was Joe Guthrie standing in a doorway. He, too, was watching Ridge and the two other men with absorbed interest. When the three of them turned into an alley and went out of sight, Guthrie started walking down the sidewalk. Once again Ben moved back into the shadows until Guthrie had passed.

It was at least ten minutes before Ridge came back to where Ben was waiting. "We talked it out," he said, "an' we agreed not to cause each other no grief. They said they jus' come into town for a drink an' would be ridin' out soon, but I still don't trust 'em. We'd best stay sober tonight an' keep an eye out for our backsides."

"Did they say anything about bein' the ones hidin' out up in the mountains?" Ben asked.

"Not directly, but they said Firston was lettin' 'em come down one or two at a time for a little fun. We agreed we'd be strangers if we ran into each other again."

"Joe Guthrie saw you talkin' to them two,"

Ben said. "He was standin' in that doorway up there."

"Ain't no law 'gainst talkin' to somebody," Ridge said, dismissing Ben's worry. "Let's head on up to that dance for a spell."

CHAPTER TEN

The building where the dance was being held served several purposes for the town. Not only was it the courtroom and town meeting hall, but it was constantly being used for other special occasions such as this dance. All the benches inside had been moved so they lined the walls, and along one side of the room a long table was loaded with food.

There were at least two men for every woman present. In one corner a small band sawed away at fiddles and twanged guitars. Ben and Ridge joined the other cowboys who stood along the walls watching the dancing.

Across the crowded room Ben saw that Joe Guthrie had joined Clarice and her parents on a bench beside the table of food. Clarice wore a long, pink dress, which set off her slim, tanned limbs beautifully. She was smiling gaily as she chatted with Joe and watched the dancers whirl by.

Joe, too, was dressed immaculately in a gray suit and vest. Ben felt a flash of shame as he looked down at his own clothes. He realized suddenly that part of the reason he had bought them was his hopes of impressing the girl, but compared to Joe's spotless appearance, he still felt shabby.

"Let's get some of that chow," Parkman suggested. "We ain't had nothin' since lunch, an' that whiskey is growlin' around in my stomach."

"I guess I'll wait a while," Ben told him.

Parkman looked at him curiously and then glanced over at the table of food. When he saw the girl he grinned knowingly and said, "That little lady ain't goin' to bite. I swear I ain't never seen such a shy hombre as you."

"I jus' don't want to eat right now," Ben snapped.

"Suit yourself," Ridge said as he started away toward the food.

In a moment Clarice and Joe got up to dance. It was a lively tune, and the girl twirled gracefully in the young man's arms. Ben tried, but he just could not seem to keep his eyes off her. When Ridge came back he had two plates in his hands. "Thought you might be jus' a little hungry but couldn't get your feet unstuck from this spot," he said, handing Ben one of the plates of food and a fork. Ben took the plate and began to eat.

When the song ended Joe and Clarice were about to return to their seats when she saw Ben. She said something to Joe, and he turned to go sit down as she started over to Ben.

"Hello, Ben," she said. "I didn't see you standing over here. Why didn't you come over and say hi to us?"

"We just came in a minute ago," Ben said.

"I saved a dance for you on my card," Clarice smiled at him. "I didn't know if you would come tonight, but I left a space open just in case."

"That's mighty nice of you," Ben said hesitantly, "but I guess I don't know how to dance. I'm sorry."

"That's all right," the girl said lightly. "A lot of men out here never had time to learn things like that. Dad's like a wounded buffalo when mother drags him out on the floor." She withdrew her small dance card from a hidden pocket on her skirt and looked at it. "It's three songs from now. Come over when it starts, and we'll take a walk instead."

After she had walked away, Ridge said to Ben with a grin, "You don't give yourself enough credit, pardner. That gal's a little sweet on you."

"She's jus' bein' nice," Ben said, "because of what happened the other day. You know she's goin' to marry that banker's son."

"He ain't man enough for her," Ridge insisted, "but she jus' hasn't realized it yet. Mark what I say."

Ben wolfed down the rest of his food, scarcely tasting it, and waited impatiently for the next two songs to end. Finally when the band began playing the third tune, he started hesitantly across the room.

As he neared, Harvey Morgan rose to shake his hand, and Mrs. Morgan greeted him with a smile. "Glad to see you, young man," Morgan said. "How's things goin' over on Paulson's spread?"

"We're losin' a few head," Ben said. "Mr. Paulson's had us bringin' most of the herd down nearer the ranch where we can watch 'em better."

"I got the same problem," Morgan said. "Might be we're goin' to have to ride up in them mountains an' see what kind of varmits we can flush out."

"You men can talk over work later," Clarice interrupted. "I saved this dance for Ben, and we're going to walk out and get some air."

Joe Guthrie glared dourly at Ben, but he did not venture to make any comment.

As Ben and Clarice crossed the room and went out the door, she took his arm. He felt self-conscious, as if every eye in the room were watching them, but he also felt a refreshing sense of pride that she would choose to spend a few minutes with him. Once outside, Clarice said, "I love to come to these dances, but I like to get out away from the crowd once in a while, too. It gets so stuffy and noisy sometimes that all I want to do is get out where it's quiet and I can see the stars."

"I know what you mean," Ben said. "Sometimes I wonder if people were meant to spend their lives closed up inside buildings. In the last few years I get a funny feelin' when there's walls around me for too long."

They walked along in silence for a while, away from the lights and noise of town, but it was a comfortable silence, and a feeling of contentment started coming over Ben. It was a new feeling, but he liked it, and he felt completely at ease with the girl now, away from the eyes of all the people inside. He let her set the pace and direction, and her steps led them down the road leading out of town.

A few hundred feet from the last building on the edge of town, she led him off the road into a small grove of trees. "When I was a little girl and we would come to town," she said, "Joe and I used to come out here and play cowboys and Indians in these trees. I've known him for as long as I can remember, and we've always been sort of pals and sweethearts.

"Even when we were twelve and thirteen, it was always taken for granted that we would get married some day. About four years ago when he went away to school back East, I was only sixteen, but we agreed then that when he got back we would get married. Everything seemed settled, but now. . . ." She let the sentence fade away as she collected her skirts and sat down on a fallen log. "He just came back a different person," she said finally. "All those fancy clothes and too many manners. He looks down on everybody now, and he's so jealous . . . but I guess you know about that."

"I sure do," Ben said.

"I guess he'll straighten out after he's been back for a while. . . ." She paused and looked up at Ben, who was still standing. "But I don't know why I'm telling all this to you. Sit down and we'll talk about something else."

Ben sat down on the log beside her and said, "Nights are different out here. The air smells different, and there's more stars. A few years ago, when I lived back home, I thought I'd never want to live anywhere else, but I can see now why people come West and fight so hard to make a life for themselves out here."

"I thought you must be from somewhere in the East," Clarice said tentatively. "You don't seem like someone from out here."

"Mississippi," Ben said. "My family used to have a little farm."

"Do they still live there?"

"They're all gone. Ma died several years back, an' then the war came an' Pa . . . well they sent me word while I was in the army that he got killed. Didn't know quite for sure who come by the farm an' killed him, but right in the middle of the war an' all, there ain't no tellin'. The war don't leave much behind when it passes through a place."

Sensing that Ben did not want to talk about his family, the girl said, "I thought you might be a soldier. Did you see much fighting?"

"Some," Ben said. "But I didn't desert," he added earnestly. He was anxious for her to know that much about him. "The war just sorta left me behind."

"I know you wouldn't desert," the girl said softly.

Ben was sitting close enough to her that her skirt brushed his jeans leg when she moved. He was wanting to reach out and take her hand, but then she said, "I suppose we'd better start back. Dad and Joe will be wondering . . . especially Joe."

Ben rose and offered her his hand to help her to her feet. She stood and brushed the bark and moss off the back of her dress. "It wouldn't do for somebody to see that," she said with a laugh. "People do enough talking now about the things I do."

They returned to the road and started walking back toward town. When they were about fifty yards from the town hall, several shots sounded out of sight down the street. "I'd better get back inside," Clarice said. "It sounds like the cowboys in the saloons are starting to have their Saturday night fun."

They had almost reached the door of the dance when Ridge came running up to them. "We've gotta get out of here," he told Ben breathlessly. "Those two men of Firston's I was talkin' to tried to break into the bank. The sheriff shot one of them an' the other got away, but that Guthrie boy said he saw me talkin' to 'em, an' now everybody's lookin' for us. They think we had a part in it. Everything's real confused right now, but they'll be comin' in a minute."

Ben only had time for one quick glance at Clarice. Her face showed confusion and disappointment. He tried to speak, but he could not think of anything to say and Ridge grabbed his arm and pulled him away.

"I mean we gotta go *now,*" Ridge insisted. Ben turned and ran with his friend toward the livery barn, leaving Clarice on the steps of the town hall staring after them.

CHAPTER ELEVEN

Ben spurred his horse and rode quickly out of town. He could hear Ridge close behind him, but he followed Ridge's instructions and did not wait for him. He gave his full attention to his own flight. A few shots rang out, but Ben knew the sheriff and Paulson's riders would not have much stomach for trying to shoot him and Ridge down. He was glad the road had been so well traveled that evening. It would be almost impossible for anybody to trail them or to tell where they turned off the road.

About a mile out of town Ben turned off the road and headed straight toward the mountains. He chose a spot where nobody riding the road would be able to see him and follow. He heard Ridge ride past, but that was all right. They had agreed on a meeting place in the last few hectic seconds in town, and it was probably better for them to stay separated now. It would make it harder for anyone to figure out their trail and follow them.

A short distance away from the road he began walking his horse to decrease the noise. He had not gone far when he heard several horses thundering down the road, but they too rode past. Ridge had probably intentionally drawn them away, but Ben had confidence in his friend's ability to escape. Ridge knew too many tricks to get caught.

Ben took advantage of as much cover as he could find as he made his way toward the mountains. From a distance they looked steep and forbidding, but as he drew closer he found that there was a maze of trails and draws leading steeply upward. A man could confuse a hundred pursuers in this complicated network. As soon as he found the opportunity, he began working his way west toward the hills above Paulson's ranch where he was to meet Ridge. They had agreed not to meet until the following night, but he thought he would get as near as possible while it was still dark, then hide out during the daylight.

It was a slow, treacherous ride in the darkness, but the moonlight helped him keep his horse on the trails. Ben stopped often and inspected his horse's hooves by match light, but old Rex, who did most of the ranch's shoeing, did a good job. The shoes were tightly fit and securely nailed.

By dawn Ben did not know how far he had traveled or exactly where he was, but he was not worried when he stopped and unsaddled his horse. When the light got better he could climb up on some nearby rocks and get his bearings.

He had chosen a small, steep-sided narrow draw to stop in. At one end was a small, sparse patch of grass. It was not much for a horse that had been ridden as much as his had, but it was something. At the upper end of the draw was a tangle of boulders that would do for cover if anyone discovered him and he had to fight. But he did not plan to build a fire, and he did not think anyone would find him.

He had nothing with him to eat, so he took a long drink of water from his canteen, gave some to the horse, and built a small shelter with his slicker. He slept all morning and woke sometime past noon.

His horse was whinnying excitedly and tugging at the makeshift hobble. Ben roused and drew his gun. Cautiously he eased down the draw toward the horse. For a moment Ben was confused. The horse was acting strangely, not like it usually acted when another horse or a man was approaching.

But as he neared the horse and patted his neck to calm him, he saw the source of the commotion.

A few yards away a rattlesnake was just beginning to coil defensively. Ben laughed out loud with relief. For a moment he had thought he was going to have a fight on his hands.

But a problem still remained. He could not allow the snake to live. It would eventually scare his horse away and might even kill it. Yet Ben knew he could not risk a shot. The sound would carry for a long distance down toward the valley, and the posse might still be out looking.

Ben looked around for something to kill the snake with, and his eyes settled on a boulder about as big as a man's head. He picked up the rock and cautiously approached the snake. It was fully coiled now and ready to strike. With all his strength Ben threw the rock. It broke the snake's back and crippled him. With another rock Ben finished the job. He walked over and picked it up. It was still writhing, but its head was crushed and it was dead.

He eased by the still skittish horse and carried the dead snake back up to the upper end of the draw. With his sheath knife he cut off the head and rattlers and slit the body up the belly. After gutting and skinning it, he cut the meat into thin strips and laid them in the sun on the rocks around him to dry.

He was not really anxious to eat raw snake meat, but he reminded himself that he had eaten worse, a lot worse, and his growling stomach reminded him that it had been some time since his last meal. He ate perhaps a third of the snake and let the rest lie in the sun to dry. He could not be sure when his next meal would be, and that night or the next day he might be glad to have it along.

After his meal he risked a smoke. It was something Ridge had warned him against. The smell of a cigarette carried farther than a man would think, and it could be enough to tip off a nearby enemy. After the smoke he dozed the rest of the afternoon until dusk approached.

When it had become fully dark, Ben saddled up and left. He had checked out the terrain earlier and knew about where he was and which direction to ride. After a couple of hours of navigating the dark, narrow, mountain trails, he decided to cut down to the valley and risk riding out in the open.

He reached the meeting place about

midnight. It was a small grove of trees and thick brush beside a stream. A couple of weeks before as he and Ridge had been herding a few strays out of the grove, Ridge had told him to remember the place in case they ever needed a spot to meet.

Ben approached the trees cautiously. When he heard the click of a pistol hammer, he said, "It's me, Ridge."

"You damn fool," Ridge hissed angrily from the darkness. "I ought to shoot you anyway for ridin' out in the open like that." Ben rode his horse into the edge of the trees and started to dismount. "Don't bother gettin' down," Ridge said. "We've got to be to hell an' gone shortly. They're combin' these hills for us. They want us bad now that they think we're part of that bunch up in the hills."

Ben followed silently as Ridge led the way up an obscure path toward the mountains. He felt surprised, humiliated, and angry at Ridge's sudden anger. He had never seen him mad before, not even when he was about to get in a fight. But Ben realized how stupid it had been to seek the easy ground in approaching the meeting place. If anyone had seen him, they could have followed him and easily caught both him and Ridge.

It seemed like Ridge was choosing the

most difficult paths that the horses could manage. Every time there was a choice of easy riding or hard, Ridge turned invariably to the hard. The posse would really have to want them to work out this trail. They rode all night, pushing the horses until they were stumbling with fatigue and Ben was about to fall out of the saddle. A couple of hours before dawn they reached the crest of the mountains, and by dawn, when they stopped, they had worked their way halfway down the opposite side.

For the first couple of hours of the ride, Ridge had stayed angry. Then he began to talk a little, telling Ben to watch out for a tricky rock or a low overhang, and finally toward morning he had loosened up and began telling about his own escape.

There was a reason for his irritability. In his pranks and tricks to elude the posse he had almost been caught. In his doubling back and hiding his trail he had confused the posse so much that they had split up in twos and threes to look for him. While twisting and turning to put off one bunch, he had ridden right up on another.

It was only the wildest luck that the men he faced were Curley, Rex, and Vegas. All three had their guns out and had him cold before he even saw them. There had been a moment of cold silence, and then suddenly Curley had growled, "Aw, hell!" and holstered his pistol. A moment later the other two had done the same, and Ridge had turned and left without a word. "Can't figure it out," Ridge said, "but I guess we got a few friends down there yet. It's nice to know in a tight spot that they're not all against us."

"Well, it don't matter to me," Ben said. "I decided on the way up here that I'm goin' after Salem an' then light out of here."

"Seems like the thing to do now, I guess," Ridge agreed. "Want some company?"

"Shore," Ben said, "but don't forget, he's mine when we get to him."

"I guess I've known that all along," Ridge grinned. "But let's stay here a while an' let things cool before we go. Anyway, I couldn't leave now if I wanted to. My gut's so empty I could eat a rattlesnake."

Ben laughed out loud. "Jus' so happens . . ." he said, reaching for his saddlebags.

CHAPTER TWELVE

That afternoon during a short scouting trip, Ben discovered where Firston and his men had been camped. He went back to get Parkman, and together they checked the site out. The camp was in a wide ravine at the head of a small valley. There was a scattering of trees around the area and enough grass for a few horses to feed on. At various places under the trees were small stick frames where Firston's men had stretched their slickers to protect themselves from the rain.

Parkman walked over to one of the piles of ashes where a campfire had been and kicked it with his foot. Buried a few inches deep were some live coals. "I'd say they left last night or early this mornin'," he speculated. "Probably 'bout ten of 'em."

"They must have took off about the time the one who tried to rob the bank got back here," Ben said.

"I reckon."

"I wonder why they left?" Ben asked.

"I don't know," Ridge said. "Looks like they rode up the mountain like they were headed over toward the valley. Maybe they decided the time was right to move on Salem."

A frown came to Ben's face when he thought about that possibility. He stood still for a moment, staring up the mountain, then without a word walked over and got on his horse. Once mounted he waited, prancing his horse and looking back at Ridge, an unspoken question on his face.

"Hell yes, I'm comin'," Ridge grumbled, "but I hope you know we're ridin' into the damndest mess either one of us is ever likely to see. Every rancher an' all their hands are lookin' for us 'cause they think we tried to rob their bank; we're tryin' to get at a man that's surrounded himself with some of the orneriest gunfighters he can find, an' we're tryin' to outrace a gang of bushwhackers who would probably just as soon take their meanness out on us as they would on Salem himself.

"An' here we are, a boy that's been an expert with a six-shooter for at least a full six or eight weeks, an' a middle-aged bone-head that don't have sense enough to turn tail an' run to save his own neck. Hell, Ben! I don't see why we should have a speck of trouble down there!"

"Maybe it won't be so bad," Ben said, turning his horse and starting up the mountain. "I been workin' with this pistol more than any eight weeks. It's been ten at least."

Riding up the steep, twisting trails was much easier in the daylight than it had been the night before, but Ben and Parkman still rode slowly, keeping their eyes constantly scanning the rocks and cliffs above for any sign of attack or ambush. Soon after they started out Ridge insisted on taking the lead. Ben did not argue because he had confidence in Ridge's ability and knowledge. In the thick forests and swamps back home, Ben thought, it might have been different, but Ridge obviously knew more about getting around in this sort of country, and Ben was satisfied with following.

They reached the crest of the mountains by noon. They dismounted and left their horses behind some boulders while they stood looking out over the lush, green landscape below. The only buildings in sight were the distant specks that marked the location of Paulson's spread. If there were any riders down below, they were too tiny to see.

"I guess they're prob'ly still looking," Ridge said. "I don't reckon there would be any use to sneak around. We might as well ride the straightest route toward Salem's an' jus' trust our luck."

"Which way do you think Firston prob'ly took?" Ben asked.

"If he was ridin' with daylight an' wasn't in no hurry, he prob'ly rode jus' under the crest of the ridge until he got nearer Salem's. If it was at night, they prob'ly rode out in the open an' jus' killed anybody that spotted them."

"Either way," Ben said, "he's already got a good lead on us. I think you're right about headin' straight across."

"Jus' can't wait to get your tail in a sling, can you?"

"The time's finally come, that's all Ridge," Ben said. "All this waitin' we've had to do is over. I've got some dead friends who will be restin' a little easier before long."

It took them only a couple of hours to work their way down to the base of the mountains. They stopped several times to try to spot anybody in the area who might give them trouble, but nobody was in sight, and they found no indication that anybody had been in the area for some time.

Despite the tension under which they had

been living for the past few days and the urgency of their mission, it was hard for Ben to ignore the calm, sunny beauty of the valley. They rode out in the open over the rolling hills, almost defying someone to challenge them, but it was as if everyone had decided to ride out and leave the valley in the quiet state in which it must have remained for thousands of years before the first men came into it, bringing greed and destruction and death with them.

But the deceptive peace was short-lived. As they topped a short rise, they were brought back with a jolt to what bitter men had brought to the valley. Ridge saw the prone figure first and muttered a low, urgent "Ho!" which caused Ben to rein up immediately. The body was over a hundred yards away and only partially visible in the grass.

"He ain't movin'," Ridge said. "Looks like he's on his stomach an' twisted kinda funny."

"We could cut back an' skirt around him," Ben suggested. "This could be a trap."

"Could be," Ridge agreed, "but nobody knew we were comin' this way. I'm jus' curious enough that I'd like to ease down there an' find out." He dismounted and pulled his rifle from its boot. "Cover me an' I'll

check the lay of the land. If any shootin'
starts an' you see me go down, light out
'cause there won't be a thing you can do for
me."

"You know better than that," Ben said,
also dismounting and getting out his rifle.

"Well, at least don't get killed tryin' to
pull some kind of stupid rescue," Parkman
said. He started walking away, leading his
horse and using it as partial cover as he approached the body.

Ben jacked a cartridge into the chamber
of his rifle and kept his eyes constantly scanning the terrain, seeking out all the places
near Ridge where a gunman might hide.
When Ridge reached the prone figure he let
the reins drop and stooped to examine the
man. In a moment he stood up and called
out to Ben, "Come on down."

Ben started to mount and ride down, but
then decided to follow Parkman's example
and led his horse down to where the body
lay. As he neared, Ridge said "I know this
feller. He's called Pete, an' he rode for Firston. He was a real low-down hombre, but I
guess he won't be backshootin' nobody ever
again."

Ben saw that Pete had been downed with
one shot between the shoulder blades. He
was lying on his stomach, but his head was

twisted oddly. His neck had evidently been broken by his fall.

"He died goin' an' comin'," Ridge observed. "Couldn't of happened to a more deserving guy."

Ben looked around in the grass nearby and saw the hoofprints of the dead man's horse. "He was ridin' east," he told Ridge, "away from Salem's place."

"I noticed that," Ridge said. "Doesn't figure, does it . . . not unless he yellowed out an' Firston brought him down. Let's have a look around here." He walked a short distance away from the body and stopped. "There's been other horses here goin' the same direction," he said. "Several of 'em ridin' hard."

He turned and came back to where Ben waited. "Well," he said, "we could stand here all day wonderin' how ol' Pete got it, but I guess we'd just as well move on."

"I'm for that," Ben said, mounting his horse.

They found another body about a quarter-mile away. At first all they saw was an arm, seemingly reaching up desperately out of a ravine. They rode over to it and Ridge dismounted for a moment. When he got a look at the dead man, he said simply, "Jody Gruder. A real lady's man. When I first saw him I didn't think he was the type to be ridin' with Firston, but then when I saw him fight, I knew he was. When the bullets would start flyin' he'd get this kind of wild grin on his face and God help the man that got in his way."

They passed the body of one other man before they came onto the real carnage of the area. Outside the edge of a small patch of trees six men lay dead, and just inside the trees were two more.

"Ambush," Ridge declared as they rode up to the bodies. He and Ben got down and looked over the area.

"Perfect place for one, ain't it?" Ben said.

"Sure is," Ridge agreed. "Looks like a neat job. A couple of riflemen over behind those rocks, a couple in the trees, an' two or three more men on horseback to run down the ones that got away. They must have had scouts out to bring back word when anybody was comin'."

Ben and Ridge walked from body to body, looking at each one. Ben recognized a few as Firston's men, and Ridge confirmed that all were members of the gang but the two in the trees. Evidently Firston's men had gotten a few shots off before they were gunned down. But Firston's body was not among the dead. "Wonder if the ol' rattlesnake lived through this one?" Ridge said. "Be just like him to . . . maybe he's too mean to kill."

"You know, Ridge," Ben speculated. "I bet this ambush wasn't even intended for Firston. I bet it was set up to take care of any ranchers who rode over this way, an' Firston jus' stumbled into it."

Ridge chuckled grimly and said, "If that's the case, maybe there's some justice in this old world after all."

Dusk was approaching, and Ridge and Ben agreed that it would be better to get some rest and move on about midnight, but neither wanted to try to sleep near the scene of the ambush. But before they left the area, they gathered up a few items, which would be useful to them. Ben found some saddlebags, which contained some crudely dried beef, a small sack of flour, and a bag of coffee. This food was important to them since neither had eaten anything for nearly two days except the snake Ben had killed.

Ridge discovered a spyglass hanging by a string around the neck of one of the men, and he searched through the pockets of three others until he found a bag of tobacco. "I never was much of a one for stealin' off the dead," Ridge said, "but as much as these fellers did it back East, I don't think they'd think too hard of us for takin' a few things we need."

When they had mounted up and were about to ride out in search of a place to camp, Parkman took one last look at the bodies scattered around behind him. "Won't be no grass growin' on the road to hell today," he muttered.

CHAPTER THIRTEEN

Ben and Parkman found a place to stop in a small grove of trees along the bank of a creek. Though the bag of coffee looked tantalizing, Ridge vetoed building a fire, even a tiny one. And without a fire they could not make biscuits from the flour either. Sitting in the dark they gnawed hunks of the dried meat and drank tin cups of cool creek water.

"I guess we can get about three hours of sleep apiece," Ridge said. "Salem's place shouldn't be too far up ahead, but close as we are we don't want to be caught out in the open in the daylight like Firston's bunch was. You want first watch or last?"

"Might as well get it out of the way first," Ben said.

"All right," Ridge said. He spread his bedroll out in a soft patch of grass beside the creek and told Ben, "Wake me up when the moon's just about to the top of that sycamore tree over there an' I'll take over."

Ben took his rifle and made his way through the trees to a point where he could watch both ways down the trail they had been following earlier. He did not try to find a comfortable place to sit because he was so tired he was afraid he might fall asleep. For the first hour of his watch, until the moon began to rise, his vigil was more one of listening and trying to hear any unusual sounds than it was trying to see anything. Several times Ben was tempted to roll a cigarette and have a smoke to break the monotony, but he kept reminding himself that anything foolish he did would endanger not only his life, but also Ridge's.

No mistakes, he kept telling himself. Every step had to be a smart one, every move had to be just right. He willed himself to stay alert and keep his senses sharp every moment.

It seemed like enough time had passed to fill two nights before the moon finally reached the point Ridge had indicated. Ben eased back through the trees and cautiously approached the place where Ridge was sleeping. When he was still a fair distance from his friend, he called out in a loud whisper, "Ridge, wake up. It's Ben comin' into camp."

Parkman slept lightly, and when he was startled awake, he usually had his gun pointed and ready to fire as quickly as he opened his eyes.

"Yeah," Ridge said. "Come on."

Ben got his bedroll and spread it out near where his partner had been sleeping. As he piled down tiredly on the two wool blankets, he said, "It's been real quiet up till now. I hope you'll keep it that way till I can get a little rest."

"Shore will try, pard," Ridge chuckled. "If any of Salem's men come by here, I'll beg their pardons an' ask 'em to sling their lead as quiet as possible so's they don't bother you none."

It seemed to Ben that he had scarcely closed his eyes before Ridge was back to wake him up. They both bundled up their bedrolls, filled their canteens in the creek, and saddled their horses. Ben took some of the beef out of the saddlebags for them to chew on as they rode. By dawn they had found a vantage point up the side of the mountains about a half-mile from Salem's ranch. They had taken a roundabout route to reach the small shelf of rock that they chose to study their objective from.

Ridge had chosen some of the more remote and difficult portions of the foothills at the base of the mountains to lessen the chance of meeting any of Salem's men or of riding into any of the ambushes that Salem seemed to have spotted around the countryside.

Ben was beginning to realize that Salem was conducting his campaign in the valley something like he might conduct a military operation to capture the area. He had his base camp set up and reasonably secure against attack and was now apparently sending out patrols to see what sort of damage he could do to his enemy.

Even the ranch area was similar to a crude military fort. In the center, on top of a small knoll, stood the house itself. It was a formidable-looking two-story stone structure with heavy wooden shutters over all the windows.

To the rear of the house was a huge barn, also of stone, with corrals on one side. Making a rough U shape around three sides of the house were a variety of small buildings, which Ben took to be cook houses, storage rooms, and bunkhouses. About twenty feet away from all the buildings, and running completely around the area, was a stone fence about four feet high.

Ben and Parkman took turns using the

spyglass to familiarize themselves with the structures and the countryside nearby. After about an hour of this, they crawled back out of sight under an overhang and began to build cigarettes and discuss strategy.

"I'd heard people describe that place as a fortress," Ben said, "but I didn't imagine how close it really comes to bein' one. It's goin' to take something more than just bustin' in an gunnin' him down."

"I been tryin' to tell you," Ridge reminded him. "This ain't a job for no hothead to take on . . . but there's still ways to get it done. Sometimes there's places one or two men can go where a whole army couldn't get in."

They stretched out under the rocks and caught up on the sleep they had been missing for the last couple of days. There was nothing they could do until dark anyway, and they would need to be rested and alert when they finally made their play.

When Ben woke in midafternoon, he took the spyglass back up to the edge of the ledge and resumed his study of every detail of Salem's fort. He was trying to memorize everything down there, every corner he might have to duck around, every window and door he might have to go through, and every bush and tree he might use to hide behind.

About dusk Ridge joined him, and they spent the rest of the daylight hours discussing possible routes they might use to get in and out of the place. When full darkness arrived, they began to make their way down the side of the cliff by a route they had worked out earlier. They went on foot. Riding horses was out of the question because the whole distance to Salem's would have to be crossed in fits and starts, using every bit of cover available. At the base of the mountains they paused at a small stream, and Ridge began taking off his boots and gun belt.

"We're goin' to have to disguise these clothes a little bit," he said. He walked out into the middle of the stream and sat down in the cold water. After wetting down his jeans and shirt, he returned to the bank and began to cake them with dirt. "I think this mud will be about the same color as the rocks they used to build that place. It should make us harder to see."

Ben followed Ridge's example, feeling stupid for a moment because Clarice flashed through his mind as he was rubbing handfuls of dirt onto the new, red shirt he had bought to impress her. He and Ridge completed their job by coating their faces, hair, and hands with the dark brown mud. When the job was finished they stood back and surveyed each other. "Do I look as danged ridiculous as you do?" Ben chuckled.

"Wal, I'd say you look somethin' like a Saturday night drunk that took a dive out of the hay loft into the barnyard," Ridge said.

"I guess we're 'bout even then," Ben said.

After getting back into their boots and buckling on their gun belts, they continued toward Salem's. There was enough low brush and other cover so the going was not too difficult until they neared the walls surrounding the ranch.

The place they had chosen to cross the cleared area outside the wall was directly behind the barn. During their observation they had not seen any guards on the wall, but they were assuming that some were posted at night. They had chosen to approach near the barn because it was in the middle of the wall, and any guards would probably be near the corners. Also, once they had crossed the wall, the barn was nearby and would provide immediate cover. Ridge led the way, crawling on his stomach through the low grass across the hundred-yard space from the last cover to the wall. When he reached the wall he sat up with his back to it and motioned for Ben to start.

Ben made his way easily across most of the distance to Parkman, but when he was only a few yards away from the wall he began to hear voices drawing near. He flattened himself out and lay still, not even risking the moment it would take to draw his gun from its holster.

The voices belonged to two men who were strolling along behind the wall. Ben braced himself for the shot that would end his life, but their talk remained casual, and they seemed to have little interest in the guard work, which they were evidently supposed to be doing. When their voices had faded, Ben risked raising his head for a look. He could just make out the backs of their heads some distance down the wall. Parkman was crouching on the outside of the wall, his gun ready in his hand. When he saw Ben moving he motioned urgently for him to crawl on up to the wall.

When Ben reached safety Parkman whispered to him, "Man! That was too close. My ol' heart was thumpin' like a drum. I wasn't sure I could jump up an' finish both of them before they plugged you."

"I jus' froze up," Ben admitted. "I didn't know what to do. I s'pose if they'd spotted me I'd of just laid there like a log an' died without a peep."

"You couldn't of done much else," Parkman said. "But they're gone now. Let's get across this wall before somebody else comes along."

Cautiously Ridge raised his head and looked both directions down the wall. When he didn't see anyone, he leaped agilely over the wall and ran crouching to the edge of the barn about twenty feet away. Ben waited a moment and then took his turn at entering the compound. Behind the barn they found an old wagon under which to hide for a moment and discuss their next step.

"We'd best check both corners of this barn before we pick one to go 'round," Ridge said. Agreeing, Ben eased out from under the wagon and crawled to one corner of the barn for a look. Another wagon was parked along the side, and about twenty feet away was the wall of a bunkhouse. There seemed to be little cover for them in that direction. He slipped back to Ridge and told him. Ridge crawled off to the other corner and saw that going that direction would mean working their way through the corrals and disturbing the horses that were resting there.

Finally Ben thought to look up. There was a window about three-feet square almost directly above their heads. "Would the stock make too much noise if we went inside?" Ben asked.

"Shouldn't bother them too much," Ridge said. "Nobody'll prob'ly even check. Let's try it."

One by one they climbed through the window and jumped down to the soft earth floor inside. Predictably, some of the stabled horses snorted in slight alarm, but when nobody came to check them after a couple of minutes, Ben and Parkman ventured on into the main aisle of the barn.

The interior of the barn was so completely dark that from a few feet away they could scarcely make out the outline of the window through which they had entered. Ben and Parkman felt their way along the aisle of stalls, knowing that if they continued in a straight direction they were bound to reach the front door of the barn. Parkman's discovery of the front of the building was such a complete surprise that he muttered "Uhhh" when he ran into it.

They waited for a moment and had about decided that the sound had gone unheard, but then a line of light blinked on under a doorway off to the side. "Damn," Parkman whispered as he pulled his gun and moved across the aisle so the light would not strike him when the door was opened. Ben drew his pistol and crouched low behind a pile of hay.

The door finally opened, and a hunched, old man emerged carrying a lantern in one hand and an ancient shotgun in the other. He had only half-pulled on his trousers over his long johns, and he was muttering complaints under his breath as if the check was more of an obligation than because he had any suspicions of an invader in the barn.

As he walked out toward the middle of the barn, Parkman stepped quietly up behind him and deftly put his hand over his mouth as he grabbed him. Ben sprang forward and relieved the old man of his lantern and shotgun.

"Don't even think about doin' nothin' but just what you're told, grandpa," Ridge whispered. "I'm gonna take my hand away an' then you can either holler out an' die or keep your mouth shut and see a few more years."

The old man eagerly nodded his willingness to cooperate and live, and Ridge took his hand away. Ben laid the shotgun aside then turned the lamp down to a faint glow and set it back inside a stall where it could not be seen from outside. "We don't want to do you no harm a'tall," Ridge said. "But we're goin' to have to tie you up somewhere for a while."

"He might be able to tell us somethin' about the inside of that house," Ben suggested.

"Good idea," Parkman said. He marched the old man back into one of the stalls and sat him down on the hay with his back to a post. "Now talk real quiet like an' tell us how to find Salem after we get into the big house."

"Which one?" the old man ventured in a hoarse whisper.

"The big one that your boss lives in," Ridge said.

"Naw, I mean which Salem?" the old man asked.

"Lester Salem," Ben said.

"All the bedrooms is upstairs," the old man said. "There's a big, fancy stairway goin' up from the front door, an' he an' his missus sleep in the room at the top of the stairs."

"Do any guards stay inside the house?" Ridge asked.

"Some of 'em go in the kitchen sometimes for coffee, but the womenfolk don't like us ordinary hands trompin' 'round their pretty rooms." The resentment in the old man's voice was obvious.

Ben held a gun pointed at the old man

while Parkman located some rope. They tried to be merciful in tying him up so the circulation would not be cut off in his limbs, but when they finished he was completely immobilized. Ridge cut two strips of burlap bag and stuffed one in the prisoner's mouth and tied the other around his head.

When they had finished, Ridge stepped back to survey his work and said, "I'm right sorry to hogtie you like this, old-timer. I s'pect you'll do a right smart of cussin' later when somebody finds you, but just remember we could have finished you off just as easy." As nearly as he could manage, the old man nodded his head in agreement.

Before he shut off the lamp, Ben located a doorway from which to leave the barn. He slowly eased the door open a few inches and took a look out. The main house was about fifty feet away, separated from the barn by a yard full of trees. Midway between the two buildings a guard with a rifle in his hand stood leaning idly against a tree.

Ben turned and informed Ridge of the man's presence. "I don't see any way to get around him," he said.

"We can't wait until he decides to move off," Ridge said. "We're goin' to have to put him out of the way somehow."

"I guess maybe I can take care of him,"

Ben said. He got a heavy curry brush and began removing the caked-on mud from his clothes. With a piece of gunny sack he brushed most of the dirt off his head and hair. "I'll just stroll up to him an' hope he don't think who I am till it's too late."

When he had removed most of the dirt, he stepped boldly out of the barn and strolled casually toward the guard. The man looked up but did not seem to pay any particular attention to Ben as he approached. When Ben stepped up beside him, the guard finally looked at his face, but he only had time for a second of alarm before both of Ben's fists struck his face in close succession. The guard fell heavily to the ground and lay still.

A moment later Ridge left the barn and joined Ben in the shadow of the trees. He looked down at the fallen guard and said with a grin, "He'll be a month tryin' to figure out what happened to him."

Avoiding the light that came from two windows on the back side of the house, they dragged the unconscious man near the back wall and scraped a few fallen leaves over him. There was only one door on that side of the house, and it was between the lighted windows, so they eased around a corner and went toward the front.

"I hope the front door's unlocked so we don't have to go back around and bust in that kitchen," Ridge said. "We're leavin' too many folks layin' around this place. Somebody's goin' to start findin' 'em pretty soon."

"Maybe we could jus' hogtie everybody here one by one," Ben said. "We could just take over the whole place."

"Too much work," Parkman said.

There was no light coming from the front windows, and the front door was unlocked. Ridge quietly raised the latch and eased the door open. Once inside, Ben and Ridge found themselves in a small hallway. On either side were closed doors, and directly in front of them was a wide stairway leading to the second floor.

Ben was about to start up the stairway when Ridge caught his arm and halted him. "I know this is a hell of a time to mention this," he whispered, "but we ain't talked 'bout what we're goin' to do once we get Salem. How're we goin' to get out of here?"

"We could work with these," Ben said, patting the sheath knife on his belt. "An' if his wife is in there with him we'll tie her up."

"Great," Parkman said. "An' all so quiet that nobody else knows we're in the house."

"Let's hope they're asleep," Ben said.

"We'll get 'em in bed before they have time to wake up."

"Well," Parkman said with resignation, "I don't guess I have any better ideas."

They both drew their knives as they started up the stairs. They had just reached the top landing when the door in front of them opened suddenly and a woman stepped out. Surprised, Ben took a quick step back, bumped into Ridge, and sent him sprawling backward down the stairs. When he reached the bottom of the stairs he lay still.

With a shrill scream the woman jumped back into the room and slammed the door. Ben leaped forward at it, unwilling, now that he was so close, to give up his chance at Salem, but the woman succeeded in getting the door locked before Ben could reach it.

After a moment of confusion Ben decided that the only thing to do was to try to get away. He bounded down the stairs and awkwardly picked up his unconscious friend. He had taken only a couple of steps with his burden when the front door sprung open and a huge man with a double-barreled shotgun stepped in to block his way. With a victorious grin on his scarred face Janson stepped quickly forward and

bashed Ben in the side of the head with the
butt of the shotgun.

CHAPTER FOURTEEN

The gray skies were just beginning to take on their daytime blue outside the big square window of the barn when Ben began to regain consciousness. The sharp pain in his head increased when he first opened his eyes; he found it difficult to focus on anything, but in a moment he was able to make out first the outline of the window and then the silhouette of the mountains beyond.

He tried to raise his hand up to touch his throbbing forehead, but both his hands were tied tightly behind his back. Looking around, he rolled over on his back and then on his side. He saw that Ridge was lying unconscious beside him, also tied up.

They were lying in the main aisle of Salem's barn. Ben clumsily raised his head a few inches and looked around. A few feet away, toward the front of the barn, the old man he and Ridge had captured a few hours before now had the situation reversed. The old man sat on a small milking stool which leaned back against one of the center posts of the barn. He was fully dressed now and held his old double-barreled shotgun across his lap. He was lost in open-mouthed, rasping sleep.

Experimentally Ben tried to sit up and wriggle his hands free from the ropes, but all it gained him was increased pain in his head and stinging rope burns on his wrists. He lay back in exhaustion to think. The first thought that occurred to him was to wonder why he and Ridge were still alive. Considering what they had been trying to do and where they had been caught, he could not understand why they had not been killed immediately. Salem might, he thought, have it in mind to use them as hostages or try to get a ransom, but that would be futile; and with all the wealth and power that his ranch and army of men provided, he would not need to bother with such small projects anyway.

Probably, Ben thought uncomfortably, Salem was merely saving them for some sort of more entertaining death than simple shooting.

With even the slightest moves, the ropes continued to cut deeper into his wrists. He could not see behind him, but he thought he had begun to bleed from the abrasions. Finally he decided to call out to the old hostler.

"Hey, old man," he said. "Hey, wake up."

Startled, the man sat upright on the stool and snatched up the shotgun from his lap. "Whaaa . . . ?" he mumbled, looking around the barn. When his eyes stopped on Ben he said, "You shouldn't startle a feller like that. I'm liable to pull the trigger on this scatter-gun before I figger out what's goin' on around me."

"How 'bout loosenin' these ropes a little," Ben said. "They're cuttin' into my hide."

"Oh no," the hostler said. "Janson'd have my hide nailed to the wall if I went to messin' with them ropes."

"Janson?" Ben asked, suddenly forgetting about the discomfort of his hands. "Big ugly feller? . . . an' yard-dog mean?"

"Mean just don't seem to be a strong enough word," the old man chuckled. "Since he come out here with Lester Salem an' become foreman, I seen him beat a couple of men 'til they wasn't nothin' much but a bloody pulp. He's jus' the right type of man to be foreman for what Salem's tryin' to do here."

As if it were only an incidental after-thought, the old man spat off to the side, pointed at Ben with a piece of straw, and said, "Janson says he's gonna beat you to death soon's the boss gets back . . . an' he was grinnin' when he said it, like he was talkin' 'bout how he was gonna enjoy a steak dinner or somethin'. I really don't envy you none a'tall. Nosiree."

"Salem's left?" Ben asked.

"Yeah," the hostler said. "You didn't even know that, did you? It's right funny, really. You an' your pard took so much trouble sneakin' in here to kill Lester Salem, an' he ain't even been back here for 'bout a day an' a half. He an' a bunch of them hard-cases are out harassin' the other ranchers around here."

That news was almost more than Ben could take. He and Ridge had risked their lives and now would probably lose them in an attempt to get Salem, and he had not even been around.

"It just ain't right that a man like that be allowed to live," Ben stormed. "You don't know all about him an' Janson an' what kinds of things they did in the war. They shouldn't be allowed to keep on livin'."

The old man spat again, looked cautiously at the door, and then said in a low, serious voice, "I know, son. Some of us ain't too fond of this place since them two got here an' started hirin' all this frontier trash, but . . . Salem's done had to tell several of us that he don't like quitters, an' that was why Janson gave them two fellers such awful beatin's for. They'd decided to light out, an' he'd decided they wasn't goin' nowhere."

For the first time since Ben had been conscious, Ridge began to show some signs of life. He gave a low moan, and then suddenly his eyes snapped wide open and he began thrashing violently against the ropes that held him.

"Take it easy," Ben called out to him. "That's no use. They got us trussed up like a couple of prize steers ready for the iron."

Parkman stopped struggling and looked over at Ben. "What in the hell happened?" he asked in amazement. "How'd we get in this fix? Last thing I remember was us sneakin' up them stairs, an' now here we are hogtied an' ready for roastin'."

"We didn't make it," Ben said. "But that ain't all of it. Salem wasn't even up there last night when we went up. He's out ridin' someplace. This feller just told me."

"Wal, I guess that rates us first prize for stupid, don't it?"

"That ain't all of it either, Ridge."

"We don't need any more bad news, pard-ner."

"Janson's here," Ben said. "I thought I'd done him in when I escaped, but I guess I didn't bash him hard enough."

"That's just great, Ben. Now what other good news you got to cheer me up with?" Ridge rolled around for a moment, testing the ropes that held him, and then he said, "Could you spare us some water, ol' timer? I got a powerful thirst."

"Don't reckon nobody would object to that," the old man said, getting up. "An' my name's Sam Akin, by the way." He leaned the shotgun against the wall and left the barn.

Ridge quickly rolled over until his back was near to Ben and said, "Get to work on these knots. You might get one or two undone before he gets back."

Working blindly behind his back, Ben was able to loosen some of Ridge's bindings before they heard the old man approaching and had to separate. By the time Sam came back in the barn, Ben and Ridge were lying on their backs about three feet apart, as they had been when he went out. Sam set the water bucket on the ground near the two men and helped each of them drink from the gourd dipper.

"What you doin' throwin' in with a bunch like this?" Ridge asked the old man. "You don't seem like the type to care much 'bout what they're doin'."

"I reckon I don't like a lot of things that's goin' on around here," Sam said, "but they ain't let nobody pull out on 'em yet, an' I don't figger they'll start with me." He let Ben finish drinking and then took a long drink himself.

"But don't start thinkin' I'll be goin' soft on you two jus' 'cause of that," he continued. He picked up the bucket and started toward the door. "I ain't goin' to help you none a'tall. Nosiree! I'll be watchin' you every minute . . . 'cept right now when I gotta carry this bucket back an' then stop by the cook shack to get a bite of chow." He went out carrying the bucket.

"Well how 'bout that!" Ridge chuckled as he rolled over to Ben. "I guess the ol' coot ain't got no stomach for the things Salem's doin'."

Again Ben went to work on the ropes around Ridge's wrists and in a few minutes had them untied. Then Ridge returned the favor. Ridge had just begun to loosen the knots of the bindings around his ankles when they heard footsteps approaching. They quickly threw the loose ropes out of

178

sight and lay back on their hands as if they were still tied.

As Janson entered, his huge frame momentarily blocked the doorway like a dark cloud blotting out the sun. He frowned as he looked around the barn and saw that the old man was missing, but the frown changed to a fierce grin when he looked at Ben.

He walked calmly over to Ben and kicked him in the side. "I never thought I'd be lucky enough to have another chance at you, you little bastard," he said. "You thought you did me in, didn't you? Well, it'll take more than a runny-nosed yella traitor like you to do that." As he talked he kept the toes of his boots at work on Ben's side. Ben tried to brace himself to receive each painful kick with as little reaction as possible. He could see that, in his excitement, Janson was edging around so that his back was to Ridge.

Ridge did not have time to finish untying his feet, so when the time came to go into action, he merely rose to his feet and locked his arms around Janson's middle so he could not draw his gun.

"Get them ropes off your feet," he shouted to Ben, " 'cause I ain't gonna last for long like this." As Ben groped to untie his feet, Ridge and Janson were stumbling drunkenly around the barn as the big man tried to free himself. Finally they went down together in an empty stall. Janson was bellowing like a wounded bull, nearly out of his mind with rage, and Parkman was pleading with Ben to hurry.

At last Ben kicked free of the ropes and rushed to the aid of his friend. He grabbed up the first thing available, Sam's milking stool, and swung it at Janson. It glanced firmly off the big man's head, but it only seemed to increase his rage.

Ridge's grip finally broke, and Janson's arms were freed. His hand went immediately to his holster, but sometime during the struggle his pistol had fallen out. As he fumbled around in the hay trying to locate it, Ben connected again with the milking stool, but again it did not have the desired effect.

"Damn, Ben," Ridge shouted. "Hit him hard!"

"I am!" Ben insisted.

Janson gave up his search for the gun and rushed at Ben. Ben swung the stool a third time, but this time Janson swatted it aside. He got his arms around Ben and began a crushing squeeze. Ridge took a second to loosen the ropes from his feet and then launched himself across the barn at Janson's back. He looped one arm around the big man's chin, snapping his head back, and brought a knee up in a jarring blow to the middle of his back.

Janson howled in pain and went limp for a moment, releasing Ben. Ben drew back and swung his fist with all his might at Janson's chin. When the blow connected, the big man finally went down to stay. Ben dropped to his knees and drew the sheath knife from Janson's belt, but Ridge grabbed his arm before he could deliver the fatal stab.

"That ain't the way," Ridge said. "Stop a minute an' cool down."

"I owe him," Ben insisted. They struggled briefly for the knife, but then a voice from across the barn said, "Throw it away."

They both looked up and saw Sam holding the shotgun on them. "He's right, son," the old hostler said. "Only a damn animal like Janson would kill a man the way you were fixin' to."

Ben froze for a moment, glaring angrily at Ridge and the hostler, and then relented. Ridge released his wrist, and Ben flung the knife away. Ben and Ridge rose to their feet and watched to see what the old man was going to do. He held the gun on them a moment longer, making up his mind, then walked over and handed it to Ben. As he walked to the pile of hay he said, "There's about six horses tied up outside. Ride the big red mare an' the paint, 'cause they're the strongest, but untie all of 'em and let 'em run off with you." Then, pointing to his jaw, he added, "Make it hard enough to put me out for a while, but don't thump me too hard. My ol' bones is gettin' soft."

Ridge went over to the old man, but he was reluctant to hit him. "You ain't got no time to be sentimental," the hostler reminded him. "It don't seem like nobody heard this fight, but somebody'll be along soon enough anyway."

"When this is all over, ol' timer," Ridge promised, "We're goin' to see you're fixed up with a job somewhere good." He popped the old man lightly across the chin and then caught him and laid him gently back across the hay.

When Ben stepped into the old man's room for a look out the window, he discovered his and Ridge's gun belts on a shelf by the door. He strapped on his and carried Ridge's back out to him.

"It's just like he said," Ben told Ridge. "There's six horses tied to the rail. Must be a crew was goin' to ride out pretty soon, but nobody's in sight right now."

"Let's hit it then," Ridge said, strapping on the guns. He opened the door and dashed out with Ben following closely behind. They pulled the bridles loose on all the horses and mounted the two the old man had recommended. Then with a couple of quick shots to spook the loose horses, they rode away with the four extra animals in close pursuit.

They rode around the side of the main house to get quickly out of the sights of the men rushing from the cook shack and bunkhouses and raced out the main gate of the ranch area. Everything happened so quickly that none of Salem's men ever got a clear shot at them. They dropped in behind the loose horses and drove them hard for about a half-mile, then let them scatter off the trail wherever they wished. Ridge led the way up a narrow, rocky ravine, which led away at a right angle from the trail. Weaving through a series of draws where their trail would be nearly impossible to follow, Ridge began to circle back toward the mountains, where he and Ben had left their horses.

"It'll take them hours to figure out what went on," Ridge said, "if they ever do. I don't think it'd ever cross their minds that we'd cut back this direction."

"Once we get our own horses," Ben said, "I want to head on down the valley. I want a crack at Salem before he gets back to that fort of his."

"Seems like the best idea. But now we've got even more hombres out after our hides. I reckon that now 'bout anybody in the valley would be tickled to throw some lead in our direction."

"By now they're probably too busy fightin' each other to pay much attention to us."

"Mebbe so," Ridge said skeptically.

By the obscure route that Ridge chose, it took them nearly two hours to reach the small, hidden ravine where they had tethered their horses. They freed the horses they had taken from Salem's ranch and then rested for a few minutes before saddling up their own animals and starting toward town.

CHAPTER FIFTEEN

Sitting on a rolling grassy hill in some of the best grazing land on the north side of the valley, Ben and Parkman sat silently watching the smoke rise from what had once been a small ranch house. It was the headquarters of one of the smallest ranches in the area owned by a man named Matt Cumberland.

Ben had met Cumberland only once in town. He was a short, stocky, red-faced man of about thirty. He was not married and lived out here and ran his ranch with the aid of only two cowboys. In the few minutes Ben had once spent drinking with Cumberland, he had quickly understood that this ranch was a total obsession with the man. To him no other world existed beyond the area where his cattle and horses grazed.

Now the carcasses of several dead horses dotted the corral area, and dozens of dead, bloating steers lay scattered on the hills sur-

rounding the ranch. More than a few marks-
men had had their fun at the extreme
expense of Cumberland.

"It's started for real now," Ridge said,
finishing a cigarette and bringing it up to
his mouth for a quick lick. "They're probably ridin' from ranch to ranch killin' and
burnin' everything in sight. I just hope the
ranchers can get together in time to stop
them. If they don't face Salem in a group,
he'll wipe everybody out a little bunch at a
time."

"How can they get away with it?" Ben
asked in amazement. "Where's the law?
Where's the army?"

"There's not much army out this way
'cause of the war," Parkman said. "An' the
troops that are here have their hands full
with the Injuns farther west. You met the
law in town, and besides him, there's probably only a handful of marshals roamin' the
territory. The only real law out here is in
the minds of the people that live here, an'
the only real enforcin' that gets done gets
done by the same folks."

"Whatever the law is out here," Ben said,
"it don't look like it's workin' too well."

"We'll have to see 'bout that," Ridge said,
taking a deep draw on the cigarette. He took
the spy glass from his saddlebags and took

a close look at the land around the ruins of the ranch house. When he had finished the examination he said to Ben, "I guess we'd better ride down. It looks like there might be a body lyin' down there."

It took Ridge and Ben nearly an hour to bury Cumberland and the one dead cowboy they found near the house. Neither could think of any very appropriate words to say over the graves, but they did stand silently nearby for a moment before mounting up and riding out. Ridge estimated that the raid had been about two or three hours earlier. They decided to follow the trail of the raiders to see where they would hit next, but they knew that more caution than they had been using would now be necessary. Salem undoubtedly had a rear guard out, and Ben and Ridge did not want to stumble into the kind of fight they would have on their hands if Salem discovered their presence.

As they followed the clear trail of Salem and his many riders, Ben was unusually silent and pensive. When Ridge finally asked him what was bothering him, he said, "We just buried a man that didn't want nothin' at all out of life but to raise a few cows an' live in peace. I've seen lots of men die for a lot of reasons, but there just wasn't any sense in this Cumberland killing. No sense a'tall . . . sometimes I think I hate Salem so much that it'll eat me clean up before I can even get to him."

"Gettin' him is one thing," Ridge said, "but lettin' him ruin you at the same time is a whole different kettle. There's a difference between revenge an' justice, an' I was hopin' that we both really had justice on our minds."

"I want him dead," Ben snapped. "Later I'll worry about puttin' names on all the reasons why I killed him." Something about the way Ridge had spoken irritated him. They had been together for some time now, and all along he had thought that they were both of exactly the same mind. Now he was not so sure. Any other time, with any other cause, he would have been much more receptive to talk about such things as justice, but he did not want any maybes when it came to the subject of killing Salem.

After about an hour's ride east they began to watch a distant column of smoke rising lazily over the hills. They rode on with dread, knowing far too well what they would find when they reached the next small ranch. They quickened their pace, but as they neared the point where they might possibly be seen from the hills near the ranch, they cut away from the trail of Salem's men and approached from another side. They suspected that they were moving faster than Salem and his men were, and they were afraid that some of the marauders might still be around finishing up the job.

But when they eased up the side of a hill overlooking the ranch, no one was in sight below. Ridge produced the spyglass and looked the area over, carefully. There did not seem to be anybody hiding anywhere, and he couldn't detect any bodies either.

A middle-aged couple named Trent owned the ranch. They were friends of the Paulsons and had occasionally visited the Paulson ranch, so Ridge and Ben knew them slightly. Theirs was a small ranch, too, but they kept three hired hands on the payroll and produced some of the fattest, most prime cattle in the valley.

"Maybe the Trents got wind of Salem somehow an' got out," Ridge said hopefully. "Either that or somebody'll find their bones in the ashes of the house."

When they rode down, the coals of the house ware still too hot for any close investigation, but they did look in the barn and corrals and found no dead horses. Their hopes rose that everyone had left before Salem struck.

"Maybe someone's ridin' ahead an' spreadin' the word," Ben said.

"I sure hope so," Ridge said, "because the only way Salem's goin' to be stopped is if all the ranchers get together an' meet him head-on."

"It's goin' to be bloody," Ben said.

"I reckon so," Ridge agreed. "Looks like this one's shapin' up to be right messy."

With no burying to do, there was little reason for them to tarry at the Trent ranch. Dusk was approaching as they rode out, and Ridge began to quicken the pace. Salem's men were not far ahead now, and they decided that it would be better to risk a little fast riding while there was still daylight left rather than try to follow the trail in the dark.

But their worries about detection were not necessary. After riding hard for nearly an hour, they began to hear the rattle of distant gunfire, and they knew that Salem and his men were fully occupied in the third of their destructive attacks. The territory they were crossing was unfamiliar to Ben because most of his riding outside of Paulson's ranch had been restricted to the main road and the mountains, but as they neared the gunfight he suddenly became sickeningly aware of whose ranch was next in line for Salem.

"That's the Morgan place, isn't it?" he asked Ridge with alarm.

"I reckon it is."

In the gathering dark they approached on horseback as near as they dared, then dismounted and went forward on foot. Topping a hill above the Morgan ranch Ben saw a scene below that was uncomfortably reminiscent of scenes he had seen many times in the war. No lights burned in the ranch or bunkhouses, but about five hundred yards away, in a wide circle around the buildings, at least a dozen campfires boldly lit the night. The distorted images of several men were visible around each fire.

"I didn't figure on so many," Ridge said in amazement. "Must be fifty at least, maybe sixty."

"But it looks like they're still holding out at the house," Ben said. "I wonder why Salem hasn't tried to burn them out yet?"

"Probably couldn't get near enough in the daylight," Ridge said. "I expect they'll try it after it gets full dark."

"We've got to do somethin'," Ben said urgently. "Clarice an' her mother might still be in the house, an' I don't think Salem's men would blink an eye at shootin' down women."

"It's a good idea, but right off I don't see

much we can do 'cept go down there an' get shot up tryin' to be heroes."

"I don't know what," Ben said, "but I'm goin' to try somethin'. I can't jus' lay here an' watch the Morgans get wiped out."

"Okay, Ben. We both know we're goin' to do somethin', but let's jus' take a minute an' think this thing out before we go off half-cocked an' do somethin' stupid."

"All right, Ridge, do your figgerin' an' let's get a move on."

"The first thing is, if we both go down there right now, even if we do make it through to the ranch house, it'll only mean that we get burned out when Morgan an' his family does. One of us has to go try to round up some help from some of the other ranchers. I guess they haven't heard that Salem's on the rampage or they'd be here already."

"You go," Ben said abruptly.

"All right," Ridge said, "but there's a couple of other things to think about, too. One is how to keep Salem from burnin' Morgan out before I can get back with help."

"The only way to slow them down will be from inside their circle, where there's some help," Ben said. "But with as many men as Salem has here, if he wants to burn that

192

house down, he's gonna burn it."

"I reckon so," Ridge said. "But one break is that the moon will be up and full for a few hours tonight. As clear as it is around the ranch house, it should be hard for anybody to get very near without bein' seen. But that will also mean it'll be hard for you to get near without bein' shot yourself."

"I'll make it in."

"I hope so, but how to do it will be a problem you'll have to face when you get down there."

"So that settles it," Ben said, rising and picking up his rifle. "You're goin' for help an' I'm goin' down there."

"I guess that's it," Ridge said. The two men stood facing each other for a moment, each aware of how likely it was that they might never see one another again.

"I've had a few close friends . . ." Ben began, but he did not know quite how to finish, and he could see from Ridge's face that no more words were necessary anyway. Silently they shook hands, and then Ridge turned and started toward where they had left the horses.

As Ridge's shadowy form faded away in the darkness. Ben turned and started walking boldly down the hill. He decided that he would stand a much greater chance of discovery if he tried to sneak through Salem's offensive line than if he merely walked through as if he was just another of the raiders. As many men as Salem had in the raiding party, the chances were good that anybody who saw him would just assume that he was a new recruit.

When he was within about fifty feet of one of the fires, he veered to one side of it and continued to walk. He made no attempt to walk quietly or to keep his movements from being detected. The men around the fire were intent on roasting some meat, which was probably one of Morgan's beeves, and they paid no attention to him.

After he was well within Salem's ring he began to be more cautious about his movements. He was in a very dangerous zone for a while because the rifles from either opposing side would be able to reach him. When he was about a hundred yards from the ranch, a shot came from that direction, and a second later the bullet kicked up a handful of gravel about three feet to his left. Ben dropped like a stone and quickly rolled sideways until he was out of sight behind some brush. In the still night he heard the lever action of a rifle being cocked.

After a moment of waiting and listening, trying to detect anything around him that might mean an immediate threat, he began to crawl cautiously forward. There was enough low brush to conceal him as he crawled, but it was impossible to do so silently. When he decided he must be near the edges of the ranch area, he began to pause every few yards and call out in a loud whisper that he was a friend and wanted to come up. There was no use, he decided, in trying to get near secretly, because he stood a much greater chance of being shot if he startled someone than if he announced his presence to the guards.

Finally his call was answered by a cautious voice ahead. "Who are you?" the voice asked suspiciously.

"I'm one of Paulson's hands," Ben said. "I came in here to help you hold off the raiders. My partner has gone for help."

"Allright, mister," the man said. "Stand up and keep your hands in sight while you come in."

"I've got a rifle with me, an' I don't want to leave it layin' out here," Ben said.

"Just hold it by the tip end of the barrel and don't make no sudden moves a'tall 'til you get up here where we can look at you," the man said.

Ben stood up and followed the man's instructions. He held both hands up in plain view, grasping the barrel of the rifle with one hand and keeping the other hand open where they could see that he held nothing in it. He saw no one until he had walked right up into the ranch yard. The one man who had been crouching down behind a watering trough and another who had been behind a tree both revealed themselves and came up to him. One took the rifle from him and the other took his pistol from his holster.

Ben counted himself lucky that he did not recognize either of the men, and they did not seem to know who he was. Considering the ugly mood that they and every other person on the ranch were likely to be in, he figured that if they realized he was one of the two men who had fled the night of the dance, they would probably have shot him on sight.

"Mr. Morgan knows me," Ben offered. "Let me talk to him, an' he'll tell you I'm on the square. I just want to help you hold off Salem an' his bunch 'til my pard can get back here with some of the other ranchers an' their men."

"I'll take him in, Carter," one of the men told the other. "You stay out here on guard."

The man who had been behind the trough gave Ben's rifle to his friend and then returned to his post. The other man motioned with his gun toward the house and said, "Let's go."

They walked over to the front of the house, but before they could mount the steps up to the porch, the man halted Ben. He called out to the house, "Mr. Morgan. We got a man out here says he knows you an' come to help us."

In a moment the heavy, wooden front door of the house opened, and Harvey Morgan stepped out onto the porch. No lights were visible inside the house behind him, but Ben could see the shadowy form of someone behind him just inside the doorway, and he thought it was Clarice. Morgan crossed the porch and only recognized Ben when he got to the edge.

"You," he said sternly. In the faint moonlight Ben could see no expression on the man's face. "Why would you care anything about helping us?"

"Everybody's got it all wrong about Ridge and me," Ben said. "If you'll give me a few minutes I'll tell you about the whole thing from the start."

"I don't have no truck with bank robbers," Morgan said unemotionally, "an' I don't need help from murderers an' outlaws. You saved my daughter's life once so I won't let my men do nothin' to you, but I don't want you on my place." He told Ben's guard, "Let him go back out the way he come in." He turned away and started to go back inside, but Clarice's voice behind him made him stop.

"Why don't you hear him out, dad?" she said. "I think you owe him that much no matter what you may think of him."

Morgan stared in the direction of his daughter for a moment, then turned back to Ben and said, "All right, I'll listen, but I don't think you can convince me of anything. I saw you run that night they tried to blow up the bank." He asked the man who was guarding Ben, "Have you got all his guns?"

"Yessir," the man said. "He's disarmed 'cept for his sheath knife."

"Give him your knife, Halpert, an' then come on in," Morgan said.

Ben gave the knife to the cowboy and followed Morgan into the house. Clarice had stepped back into a doorway and did not speak as he walked past her. Ben could vaguely make out that she was dressed in pants and a dark shirt. He could see the light features of her face but could not make out any expression. As Morgan led the way

into a rear room of the house, she followed
along.

CHAPTER SIXTEEN

The kitchen that Morgan led them into had heavy blankets hung over the windows, and a lamp, which had been trimmed down to a dim glow, burned on the table. He went to the stove and got himself a cup of coffee but did not offer Ben any. Clarice poured two more cups and brought one to Ben.

"Sit down there an' start talkin'," Morgan said, seating himself at one end of the long dining table.

Ben sat down and took a drink of the coffee. He had decided to tell Morgan everything, but he did not like the idea of Clarice hearing it all, too. He was not proud of the fact that he had been a convict, and he would rather her not know about it, but he knew he was in no position to tell her to leave the room. And anyway, she was the real reason he was being given a chance to speak, so he decided that she was entitled to hear his explanations of the circumstances that had brought him unjustly under suspicion.

As Ben started to tell his and Ridge's story, he could tell even from the first that Morgan's attitude was softening. He sensed that the older man really wanted to believe him and trust him, but with the situation in the valley what it had been for the last few months, he had grown accustomed to believing and trusting practically nobody.

Instead of the disgust he had expected on Clarice's face, when he told of being in prison and of his living in such a brutal way, he saw compassion in her eyes as her imagination went to work on the horrible scenes he described. The only thing he found himself hiding from the girl and her father was the real intensity of the hatred he felt toward Salem. Somehow he was just too ashamed of his deep desire to kill to reveal it in its full intensity.

Finally he got around to the events of the last two days and began telling about the two burned-out ranches he and Ridge had passed on their way here.

"We been expectin' somethin' like this to start for weeks now," Morgan said, "but still when it started it was so sudden that it caught us off guard. They ringed around us out there so fast that we didn't have time to send even one rider out to bring back help. I sent one man out to try to get through, but it's been several hours and I don't think he made it."

"They won't get Ridge," Ben said with conviction. "He's slick as an Injun. I just hope somebody will believe him when he starts tellin' about what's goin' on out here. Some help's goin' to have to get here fast, 'cause when the moon goes down they'll start tryin' to burn you out." He said that before he even thought about what effect it might have on the girl, but when he glanced over at her, instead of fear he saw the same cold determination to fight that was on her father's face.

"I was thinkin' the same thing," Morgan said. "They've lost quite a few men tryin' to get close enough to torch us. I've got seven hands out in the yard an' two more up on the roof, an' they've been able to spot anybody that gets very close, but when the moon goes down we've got real problems."

"I had an idea . . ." Ben said. "It might not be too good, but maybe it could buy you a little time if you need it."

"I'm about ready to try anything," Morgan admitted. "All I've been able to come up with is to just try to take as many of them with us as we could."

"It might not have to end that way," Ben said. "Salem's a military man, an' from what I've been able to see of the way he's operated so far, it looks like he prefers the military way of doin' things. That makes him predictable . . . I hope." He finished the coffee in his cup, and wordlessly Clarice got up to refill it for him.

"When he makes his attack," Ben continued, "I don't think he'll just send in a few men to try to sneak up an' burn you out. He'll mount a full charge with all he's got. He must know you haven't got very many men, an' he'll figure on wipin' you out in one quick sweep."

"So what can we do about that? If he gets close enough so that all my men are forced to draw back into the buildings, all he'll have to do is burn the buildings down on top of us."

"You could give him fire for fire," Ben said. "I just crawled through the brush around here an' saw how dry it is. If you put the torch to it an' the wind helps out a little, it should give Salem's men all they can handle for a while just to keep from burnin' up. It might buy you an hour or two, an' that's what you should try to think about right now, just holdin' out 'til dawn comes or help gets here."

"But what about the cattle?" Clarice asked with alarm. "That could start a range fire that . . ."

But her father interrupted her before she could finish the sentence. "We're just worryin' about stayin' alive right now, honey," Morgan said, patting her hand gently. "I'd personally shoot every steer on my range if it meant savin' yours an' your mama's life."

There was a knock on the back door of the kitchen, and Clarice quickly spread a black cloth over the lamp. When it was covered Morgan drew his pistol and said, "Come in." The door opened and two men came in, closing the door behind them. Morgan seemed to recognize them because he reholstered his gun as they went toward the stove to get coffee. It was not until Clarice took the cover off the lamp that Ben saw that one of the men was Joe Guthrie.

"There's biscuits and meat in the oven," she told them, and because they were busy getting food for themselves, it was a moment before young Guthrie realized Ben was in the room. When he did finally turn around with a cup of coffee in one hand and some food in the other, he froze for a moment, incredulous at seeing Ben sitting at the table.

He was totally confused, and clumsily he

started to put down what he was holding as if about to go for his gun. But Clarice's sharp command cut him short. "Don't start that again, Joe," she said. "It's getting too tiresome."

"How did you catch him?" the banker's son asked.

For the first time Ben began to get an idea of what Morgan seemed to think of his future son-in-law. There was very little patience in his voice when he said, "Ben's come in to help us, an' he's got an idea that just might save all our hides."

Guthrie started to sit down at the table as if he wanted to participate in the planning, but Morgan told him, "We need every man out there on guard, Joe. You two take your food and coffee back outside an' keep watchin'. We'll tell you what's goin' on when the time comes." The young man started to say something, but Morgan cut him off by rising and saying to Ben, "Come on. Let's go outside an' look around. We need to figure out if this plan of yours will work without us burnin' our own selves out first."

Morgan led the way back through the front of the house, and after they left the kitchen Ben briefly heard Joe and Clarice's voices rising angrily behind them. But they were outside before he caught the drift of the argument. Ben found his two guns and knife laying on the porch. It felt good to drop the pistol back into its holster and to hold the rifle in his hands again.

As they walked around the ranch area, Ben saw that Morgan had placed his few men wisely and that they were covering every possible angle of approach to the house. And the two men with rifles on the roof of the house, who had an unobstructed view in every direction, were good added insurance. If Salem did mount an attack on the place, it would be costly to him. Still, Ben knew, it could be taken. There were just too few men to hold out for very long. What he saw deepened his conviction that the fire would have to work and that Ridge would have to line up some help quickly or none of them would probably ever see daylight again.

There were only a couple of places where setting a grass fire might threaten any of the ranch buildings, and the two men agreed that one man in each place with wet bags and shovels would be sufficient to keep the buildings from being burned. But there were other problems. The wind was blowing gently to the east, and the fire would have difficulty on the western side of the ranch. Ben and Morgan agreed that coal oil would have to be used and that the defenses would have to be concentrated on the west side to take care of any of the raiders who got past the flames.

Their other problem was knowing exactly when to set the fires. If they waited until the attack had actually started, the flames might not have time to get strong enough to be any protection, but if they set it before the attack, all Salem's men would have to do is wait until the fire had burned itself out or was at least far enough away from the ranch buildings before beginning the assault.

When their inspection was finished Morgan got one of his hands to begin filling jars and tin cans with coal oil. While Morgan was issuing instructions, Ben returned to the house to get some food and more coffee. He knocked on the back door as he had seen the other men do, and in a moment he heard Clarice say, "Come in."

After he closed the door Clarice uncovered the lamp and returned to the stove where she was frying meat. "I thought you would be hungry," she said with a smile. "How long have you been in the saddle?"

"Seems like it's been a month," Ben said, "but I guess it's only been since this morning."

"You look dead on your feet," she said. "And you really ought to let me do something about that cut on your face."

Ben raised his hand to the side of his head and touched the place where Janson had bashed him with his rifle butt the night before. He was startled to find how sore it was and to feel dried blood flake off under his fingers. With things happening as quickly as they had all day, he had completely forgotten about the wound.

"I bet I'm a sight right now," Ben grinned.

"Aren't we all," the girl said lightly. Unconsciously she raised a hand to brush back a stray wisp of hair, which had fallen over her face.

Ben got a cup of coffee and sat down in one of the chairs at the table, but he knew he should not sit for long. His body just seemed to settle when he relaxed, and he could feel the tiredness flowing through his body, begging for rest.

With her back turned, Clarice said, "I'll have something ready for you in a minute. I've been cooking all night for the men. The cook's out on guard, and all of this was just too much for mother. She tried to help, but we finally made her go upstairs and lay down."

"When the fighting starts you'd better get

her back down here an' near some outside door. If they set fire to this house, she might get trapped if she's still upstairs. Just inside the first room might be a good place for you an' her to hide out while the bullets are flyin'."

"I'm too good a shot to be hiding anywhere," Clarice said. "I'll bring mama down and put her where you said, but I've already got my window picked out." She turned and indicated one of the back windows of the kitchen where a rifle leaned against the wall.

As she finished her cooking Ben watched her, feeling a little guilty and frustrated by the thoughts that entered his mind. He kept trying to remind himself that this nearness and friendliness meant nothing, but it was hard for him to drive out all the natural dreams and wants that he felt as he watched the slim young girl at work.

Finally, she forked the last of the meat onto a plate and brought it to the table. Then she returned and got a plate of warm biscuits from the oven. "It's simple," she said, "but at least we've got plenty. Take all you want."

"I need to be gettin' back outside," Ben said. "I'll take some with me an' eat it after your dad tells me where he wants me to stand guard." He took off his hat and began loading it up with food. But as he was starting to the door, Clarice stopped him with a question.

"Why did you risk your life to come in here and help us?" she asked. "You said that all you wanted to do was get Salem, but you would have stood a much better chance of doing that by staying out there and sneaking around his campfires until you saw him." When Ben turned to look at her, a long, still moment passed as they gazed deeply into each other's eyes.

"I never thought about it," Ben finally stammered out. "When Ridge an' I was lyin' up on that hill an' I saw what was goin' on down here, I just knew that you . . . an', uh, your family . . . was in trouble an' I had to do what I could."

Without a word the girl came to him. Crushing the hat full of food between them, she put her arms around his neck and gave him a long, full kiss. With his rifle in one hand and the food in the other, Ben felt as clumsy as Joe had seemed, not knowing what to do or say.

After the kiss Clarice drew her arms from around his neck and stepped back slightly from him. "Mother says I'm brazen," she said, "but sometimes I just do what I feel like doing without stopping to think about it." Then suddenly she seemed embarrassed, and she turned away from him slightly as she added, "And right then I felt very much like I wanted to kiss you."

Ben turned numbly and went to the door. He left without giving her time to cover the light. His mind was in a fog, and he nearly fell off the porch before he realized that he was at the edge of it. He crossed the yard to the barn and found Morgan helping a cowboy fill the cans and jars with coal oil.

Looking up from the work as Ben approached, Morgan said, "We're just about ready, but we still have to decide when to light the fires. When do you think would be best?"

"Well, I uh . . ." Ben began. He had to force his mind to return from Clarice to the business at hand. He leaned his rifle against the barn and took a mouthful of the meat and biscuits from the hat.

"Well, if our guess is right about what Salem plans to do," Ben said finally, "then he'll be giving the order to charge pretty soon. The moon's almost down, an' it's gettin' harder to see already. How about lettin' one of your men on the roof give the word just when Salem's men have mounted up an' started this direction? They should be able to watch the campfires an' tell us when all the men have left them to get their horses an' start in. That'll give us four or five minutes to get some blazes going. It might be time enough."

"Why don't you go up there?" Morgan suggested. "The way you handle that rifle. I'd hate to be chargin' any building you're on top of."

"I'll stay down here," Ben said. "I've faced a charge or two, an' I know what to do. I think I'd be more use here on the ground."

"All right," Morgan agreed. "I'll go up an' tell them when to give the word." He left to do his errand, and Ben stayed to help the cowboy distribute the materials and give instructions.

When all the preparations were made, Ben took three jars of the coal oil and took up a position behind a woodpile at the rear of the house. He was aware of someone to his left sheltered behind a spreading oak tree, but he did not realize it was Joe Guthrie until Joe made a cigarette and struck a match to light it. Still Ben said nothing. Whatever problems there were between them would have to wait until this fight was settled. Later, if they lived, something would have to be said or done. But right now they were on the same side fighting for the same reasons.

Somehow Ben had expected a long, anxious wait before the action began, but he had been in position scarcely five minutes when Morgan's voice boomed out over the stillness, "All right, boys. Light 'em up. Here they come!"

Ben snatched up his jars of coal oil and rushed out into the brush about thirty feet away. Pouring out the precious stuff sparingly, he scattered the coal oil over the brush and thick, dry grass in a fifty-foot line parallel to the position he had chosen to defend. When he was finished and tossed a match to the ground, the flames seemed to spread with agonizing slowness. But during the moment he watched, the fire crept slowly along the ground, and soon the heat was so intense he was forced to step back several paces.

Looking to his left and right he saw the fires that the other men had set spreading out in both directions. As he turned and jogged back to the woodpile, his hopes began to rise that the fire might really have time to gain the strength it needed to hinder Salem's charge.

Ben had chosen a position on the west side of the ranch because he knew that the fighting would be the heaviest there, but he had not figured on having to contend with the smoke that the breeze was blowing in his direction. Soon the air was so smoky he had difficulty in seeing young Guthrie behind his tree twenty-five feet away.

The flames were spreading quickly, but before long, over the crackling of the fire, he heard the first terrifying sounds of thundering hoofbeats approaching. He felt the all-too-familiar, nauseating wave of panic flash through his body he had felt so many times before, but he fought it back, as he had taught himself to do in the war, and waited.

When the sound of pounding hooves, complaining horses, and shouting men had grown so intense it seemed they must be right on top of him, the rapid-fire staccato of Guthrie's rifle began to ring out. Ben knew that the riders were still too far away to see, and it aggravated him that Joe was wasting ammunition. But the shooting lasted only a moment before the rifle was empty, and then Ben turned in time to see the young man flee in terror toward the house.

The first shadowy form of a horse and rider was nearly on top of Ben before he could make it out. The smoke was so thick that the rider rode his mount straight at the woodpile without seeing it. Ben fired, and

214

the same moment the rider began to fall from the saddle, the horse saw the barrier and swerved so suddenly it fell. The dead rider was thrown clear and landed on top of Ben. In a scramble Ben extricated himself from the tangle and, coughing and gagging from the smoke, tried to spot the next attacker.

Ben could tell that few riders were getting through the wall of flame because by rights there should have been more men coming through than he could handle. But in a moment another form emerged from the white smoke, and Ben fired three times before he toppled the man from the saddle.

But the smoke had become unbearable. His eyes were watering so badly he could no longer see, and he was coughing so much that he knew he would have to seek refuge and a few breaths of good air if he were to stay conscious much longer. Blindly he began stumbling away from the woodpile. Another rider nearly rode over him, and two shots rang in his ears, but he was untouched. He turned and fired in the direction the horse and rider had gone and was rewarded by the sound of something heavy falling to the ground. He stumbled on.

Then suddenly a wave of clean, cool air swept over him. He fell to the ground in a coughing fit that quickly turned to vomiting, but in a moment he forced himself to stop and rose to his feet. The steady rattle of gunfire mixed with the screams of dying men and animals all around to produce a horrifying din, but for a flash second, no living thing was in sight around Ben.

Then four riders emerged from a solid wall of smoke and flame, riding straight at Ben. Small flashes of flame spit from their guns as they fired at him, but he fell and rolled quickly to one side to avoid their bullets and the pounding hooves of their homes. As they passed he drew his revolver and fired until it was empty. Two of the saddles were empty as the horses disappeared back into the smoke in the direction of the house.

Ben holstered the empty revolver and fumbled around on the ground until he found his rifle. Shots were still being fired from inside the wall of smoke, but he knew he would be of no use if he tried to go back in there. He ran crouched down to the porch of the house and found temporary protection behind one of the thick posts that supported the porch roof. Using the railing around the porch to steady his weapon, he began to methodically eliminate every man on horseback who came in sight. Someone was firing from a window about fifteen feet away, but he never bothered to look around and find out who it was. He assumed it was either Clarice or Guthrie.

Then, almost as suddenly as the hellacious fighting and killing had begun, the shooting slowed to an occasional sharp report and then stopped altogether. The fire was quickly growing in intensity, but it was also getting farther from the ranch buildings, and the smoke was not as thick as it had been originally

Finally Ben rose and took a few cautious steps into the yard. A sudden change in the direction of the wind cleared the yard of smoke for a moment, and he got his first glimpse of the carnage he had helped create. A dozen or more dead men and half that many dead horses lay within sight. Numbly he crossed the yard and ended the misery of one of the thrashing horses.

Gradually he began to be aware of another sound through the roar and crackle of the fire. There was shooting far off, a lot of it. Ben stopped and listened, pulling his mind up out of its tiredness and away from the sickening feeling of being a part of so much death.

Ridge had made it. That was why the attack had been so short and why he and the

Morgans were alive now. From the sound of things, the pitched battle that was going on out there was scattering out over the countryside in several directions. Salem's men were probably being routed and were taking off in individual attempts to save themselves.

Almost automatically Ben's mind returned to Salem. It would be a certainty that he would not have led the raid on the ranch house, and so his body would not be found among the dead in the yard. It was possible that he might have been caught in the surprise attack, but Ben's gut instincts told him otherwise. At that moment Ben guessed Salem was probably well into some escape plan, which he had worked out in advance.

Without waiting to check on anybody else at the ranch, Ben went to the barn and saddled the best horse he could find. As he rode out he tried to figure, to force himself to think as Salem would think, but all his mind would tell him was to ride hard toward Salem's ranch.

CHAPTER SEVENTEEN

In the distance, the intensity of the fighting seemed to be slackening. After a few minutes of riding, all signs of it were out of sight and hearing behind him. At last, Ben thought with satisfaction, Salem's own tactics of striking an adversary as he retreated were being used against him with devastating effectiveness.

Ben had no idea how long he pushed his numb body and quickly tiring horse mercilessly across country toward Salem's ranch. Riding over the gentle hills in the darkness, time seemed to have no meaning for him. It was as if he would go on this way forever, jolting along in the saddle, nearly falling asleep even as he rode, but still with only one purpose, one consideration foremost in his mind — to catch up with Salem and to kill him.

A reality seemed to start returning to him as the first light of dawn began showing in the eastern sky. He stopped once to fill the empty canteen he found on the saddle at a small creek and even allowed himself the luxury of a cigarette, but he did not dare sit down even for a moment. He no longer trusted his body to do what he wanted it to without constant urging, and he was afraid that if he started to relax at all, he would not be able to get up and go on.

As the light improved Ben began to see an occasional hoofprint headed in the direction of Salem's ranch, and he knew that his prey was doing as he had expected. But surprisingly, Salem did not seem to be pushing his horse very hard. Ben decided that Salem must be saving the animal, knowing that he might have to ride it for days and not wanting to wear it out on the first leg of his escape.

At last Ben topped a small rise and saw a man far below watering his horse. Ben turned and rode back down out of sight, then went back up on foot and took a look. It was impossible at that distance to make out the man's face, but Ben knew it was Salem. He considered trying a shot with his rifle, but then decided that he couldn't risk shooting the wrong man. Cautiously he crawled back down out of sight and shoved his rifle back down into the boot on the saddle.

Pushing Morgan's horse mercilessly, Ben began to ride in a wide arc, which would lead him around in front of Salem. It took him nearly thirty minutes, and when he did finally cut back so his and Salem's paths would cross, he found himself at the spot where Salem's men had ambushed Firston's gang a couple of days before.

An eerie feeling took control of Ben as he rode through the scattered bodies, now bloated and horrifying, and though he wanted badly to execute his prey in exactly that same spot, he could not bring himself to dismount and wait among the distorted dead men. He rode on toward Salem's ranch for about half a mile before he got down, hid his horse, and set his trap.

Time dragged by with agonizing slowness. Ben had no way of telling how long he waited by the tree, rifle in hand, for Salem, but as he stood there the sun rose fully and the sparkling dew disappeared from the patches of grass beside the trail in front of him. He began to wonder if Salem had somehow gotten past him or if perhaps he had turned off and headed in another direction to confuse anyone who might be following him. He had forgotten to get the canteen off his saddle, and he started getting very thirsty, but he did not want to walk the several hundred feet back into the trees where he had hidden the horse and risk missing Salem.

Then suddenly a single rifle shot rang out back in the direction from which Salem would be coming. The silence of the early morning became almost unbearable as Ben stood straining his ears to hear another shot, the sound of a horse, or any other indication of what was going on. Finally he could stand it no longer. He turned and ran headlong through the trees to where he had left the horse. He started off at a quick gallop but soon decided it might be disastrous to meet Salem on the trail riding so fast and slowed the animal to a trot.

Ben rounded a bend in the trail, and far off in the distance, in exactly the same place he had wanted to stop among the bodies of Firston's slain men, he saw two figures on the ground, one flat on his back and the other kneeling over the first. Tied to a tree near the men was Ridge's reddish-brown roan, and grazing quietly about fifty feet from them was the horse Ben had seen Salem watering.

After making sure that it was Ridge that was up and not Salem, Ben rode slowly and deliberately up to them. Ridge looked up and greeted Ben with a surprised, but happy, smile, but the smile faded quickly when he saw the hard lines set on Ben's soot-blackened face. "Got 'im," Ridge said. "Kind of appropriate place, ain't it?"

Ben did not answer as he dismounted and walked over to stand above Salem. Ridge had already tied Salem's hands, and blood was trickling from the shoulder wound where Ridge had shot him to bring him out of the saddle.

Salem was filthy from days of riding, and tiredness had etched new wrinkles on his fifty-year-old face, but there was still that same superior sneer on his face that Ben had grown to hate so intensely.

"You!" Salem said, showing only slight surprise when he recognized Ben. "The camp yellow-belly. I figured you would crawl off in a hole somewhere after you got away from Janson in that battle."

But Ben took no time to respond to the insults. Calmly he drew his knife and knelt over Salem. He intended to make a quick job of it, one neat slash across the throat, and then mount up and leave. Ridge, who had been standing behind Ben, barely had time to grab his friend's hand and jerk him backward. Ben swung on his friend with a roundhouse punch, but it was with his left hand, and the blow glanced off Ridge's shoulder ineffectively.

"Now dammit, Ben," Ridge began, but Ben pulled his right hand free, flung the knife to the side, and swung again. This time he connected solidly to Ridge's jaw. Ridge staggered back but still made no effort to fight back. Ben continued to move in on Ridge.

Ridge took a couple more steps backward, saying, "Listen a minute, Ben." He dodged another blow and continued, "That man's my prisoner. I've got him under arrest, and you're not going to do anything to him. We'll bring him to justice."

When Ben's flailing continued, Ridge finally stepped inside one of the wild swings and gave Ben a punch on the jaw, which toppled him over backward. Before Ben could fully regain his senses and rise, Ridge had knelt on top of him and placed his knee in Ben's throat so he could not move. "Now are you goin' to listen to me?" Ridge asked calmly.

As Ben glared up angrily at his friend, he noticed for the first time the U.S. marshal's badge that gleamed on Ridge's shirt.

"There's a couple of things I never did get around to tellin' you about, pardner,"

Ridge said. Pointing to the badge pinned to his shirt, he continued. "This is one of them. 'Bout six months ago the U.S. government sent me in to try to find out what Salem an' Firston had goin' for them in that prison camp. My job was to get enough evidence to try Salem an' Firston an' the rest of them for war crimes after they were captured.

"An' that's still my job. I got Firston last night when I rode into town. He thought nobody would know who he was, an' I just walked up behind him an' put a gun in his ribs.

"The ranchers had things pretty much in hand when I took off after this critter, an' tomorrow we'll ride out to the Running S to offer Jude Salem an' the rest the choice of surrenderin' or bein' starved out."

He eased off Ben and merely knelt beside him as he continued. "You've got such an all-fired big hankerin' to kill a man that done you wrong that you'd walk right up an' slit his throat, an' him a prisoner of the law an' hogtied an' gonna hang anyway. Right now I'm thinkin' I was plumb wrong about you all the time. I'm thinkin' that maybe you ain't no kind of man a'tall, but just the same kind of no-count as that pile of garbage lyin' over there."

"I swore I'd get him," Ben said through clenched teeth.

"Shore," Ridge said. "An' everybody knows a man's gotta do everything he swears to in his life, even if it means throwin' away the rest of his future to do it. You're one smart feller, Ben."

Ridge rose abruptly and walked over to retrieve the knife. With a quick flip he stuck it in the ground beside Salem's head. "All right, boy," he said. "Do it. Do what you swore you'd do. Kill the man that it's been eatin' away inside you for so long to kill."

Ben got up on his hands and knees and crawled over to Salem's side. His hand reached out for the knife, but his fingers never quite touched it. A bitter oath hissed out of Salem's lips, and he said, "Do it, you yella scum. I'd do it to you in a minute."

Ben looked deeply into the man's slit eyes, at the face that he had imagined so many times in his dreams, and he said, "You would, wouldn't you?" A dry, almost hysterical, laugh rose up in his throat, and, as he rose and turned back toward Ridge, it burst forth from him and echoed down the long valley filled with dead men.

CHAPTER EIGHTEEN

Ben was sitting in the saloon with Rex, Curley, and Vegas at one of the tables in the rear of the room. It was Saturday afternoon, and Paulson had allowed his men to stop working early and come into town. He told them that he thought they deserved it after the long hours they had worked and the risks they had taken recently.

It had been over a week since the battle at Morgan's ranch, and Ben had not been back there since. He had seen Clarice and her parents once since then at the day of funerals that had been held in town two days after the battle, but things had been so confused that he had done little more than greet them and receive a few words of thanks from each member of the family.

Nine cowboys from the valley, including three of Morgan's men, were buried in a group service in the main part of the town cemetery, and separate ceremonies had been held for four members of ranch families. Thirty-six others, including nine of Firston's men and twenty-seven of Salem's, had been buried beneath a long row of plain, wooden crosses outside the main part of the cemetery. Some of the hard-cases Salem had working for him were buried in nameless graves because nobody had been able to identify them even by first name or nickname.

Ben had decided to return to work for Paulson until he saved up enough money to go somewhere, anywhere, and piece back together the kind of life he wanted to live. He had been given a standing offer of work by Paulson, but he had been working for Ridge as a guard all week and had not returned to the ranch yet.

The day after the battle at Morgan's ranch, Ridge and Ben had led a large posse out to the Running S Ranch, and Jude Salem and the few men remaining there had surrendered without a fight. During the week it had been Ben's pleasure to keep a constant, watchful eye on Janson and Lester Salem as they sat tied and brooding in the town meeting hall. He had almost hoped Janson would try to escape, but the big man never did.

A few days earlier a team of U.S. marshals,

which Ridge had wired for, had arrived from Denver. Two had left for the East with Firston, Janson, and Salem as their shackled prisoners, and the rest had pulled out yesterday with the remainder of Salem's riders who had been captured, including Jude Salem, in two wagons to go to the territorial court in Denver for trials.

The atmosphere in the valley was a mixture of sadness for the good men who had died and elation that peace had finally been restored.

Ridge had been ordered back to Washington to receive his next assignment. He had offered to get Ben a job as a marshal, but Ben had not accepted. He wanted to be away from guns and violence for a while. He needed time to reorient himself to life, to cleanse the hatred and confusion and brutality from his system, and somehow he felt that the life of a lawman would not be for him.

The beer was lukewarm but good, and it felt good to be back among friends, to no longer have to run from anybody, having to watch every move and every word for fear that someone would find him out. Paulson's three hands were overly friendly, almost apologetic, toward him, and it was a new and pleasant experience to have those kinds of friends around him. They finished the first pitcher of beer quickly and had just ordered the second when Ridge strolled in through the swinging doors and came over to the table.

"I figured I'd find you in here," he said to Ben with a grin. "You'd better watch that stuff. You might start likin' it, an' the next thing you know, you'd end up like Rex an' Curley here."

"Always got a good word for everybody, ain't you Parkman?" Curley chuckled. "I bet there ain't nothin' in the world we could say that would persuade you to sit down an' have a drink with us."

"Wal," Ridge said, "I never was one to be unfriendly to folks." He took a seat at the table and signaled to the bartender to bring him a glass. "But I really had another reason for comin' over here," he continued, looking at Ben. "Somebody over at the hotel's been askin' for you, tryin' to find out where you been this last week, an' what you plan to do now."

Ben looked up, startled, but knowing who Ridge must be talking about. "Is she over there now?" he asked.

"I don't remember Ridge sayin' anything about a 'she,' " Curley jibed. "Did he, Rex?"

"Don't believe he said 'she' even one

time," Rex agreed.

"Funny thing, though," Ridge said. "Turns out it is a 'she' I was talkin' about. How'd you know, Ben?"

The teasing did not bother Ben, but he was just not in the mood to respond to any of it. During the past week thoughts of Clarice had plagued him repeatedly, and several times he had nearly mounted up and ridden out to her father's ranch to see her, but the nagging certainty of the eventual rejection he was certain she would have to show him if he told her his true feelings kept him from going.

He had continually told himself that he only felt the way he did about her because she was the first young woman to be nice to him in so many years that he had foolishly attached more importance to her than was really necessary.

He told himself that once he found a place where he wanted to settle for a while that he would find someone else and forget all about Clarice. But the nagging doubt stayed with him that if he did let her slip away without even a try, the feeling of loss would stay with him for the rest of his life.

For the benefit of his friends he did not want to appear too anxious by jumping up and rushing away to see her, but as the talk turned to other things he could not seem to concentrate on what anybody else was saying. The beer lost its flavor, and suddenly the barroom began to be unbearably hot and smoky. Finally, after a few more gulps of the suddenly tasteless beer, he gave up all pretenses and rose to his feet. "I'm going over to that hotel," he said. Something about the determination in his voice quieted any comments the others at the table might have thought of making.

As he pushed through the swinging doors and started down the board sidewalk, he was surprised to find that his walk was a little unsteady and that his head felt light. But maybe that would be good, he thought, to let her see him in a bad light, staggering slightly, thinking fuzzy, and maybe slurring his words some. It would help her understand that he was a bad risk, an unreliable man whose sour past made him unsuitable for any real lady like herself.

He was so intent on his own thoughts and on what he would tell her when he was there that he was completely unprepared when a small hand slipped through his arm and a soft voice said, "I thought you would probably be in a saloon somewhere. That's why I asked Ridge to go looking for you."

Ben stopped and looked down into

Clarice's smiling brown eyes, speechless for a moment because of the surprise and because of how beautiful she looked. She wore a light blue dress, which outlined her shapely body above and flared out into a wide, full skirt below. Her auburn hair hung in thick, shimmering waves down over her shoulders, and her face was a vision of sweet youthfulness.

"I was just going to the hotel to see you," Ben said.

"It was such a nice day I decided to stroll around town for a while," Clarice said. "I was hoping I would run into you. You haven't been avoiding me, have you?"

"No," Ben said. "I didn't even know you were in town. I've been helping Ridge. I was going to ride out to your dad's place one of these days."

The girl kept her arm linked with his as they continued to stroll through town. When they reached the edge of town she seemed to show no desire to turn around and go back, so they walked on out of town a short distance to the small grove where she had led him the night of the dance.

There were a few moments of silence between them before Clarice finally said, "I've sent Joe's ring back to him. I guess I have known for a while that things weren't going to work out, but when he broke and ran that night at the ranch . . . he hasn't had the courage to face me since then. His father seemed to understand when I asked him to give Joe the ring. Mr. Guthrie said Joe was thinking about heading back East for more schooling as soon as his leg healed."

Young Guthrie had been conspicuously absent since the night of the battle with Salem's crew. Ben had only found out the next day that, ironically, after Joe Guthrie had panicked and bolted from his defensive position at the beginning of the attack, he had been hit in the leg by a stray bullet, which went through the wall of the house as he crouched down in a corner of the kitchen.

"I guess I shouldn't say anything about him," Clarice continued. "He's been away from Trinity Wells for so long, I guess he's just not used to the way we have to live out here. He never had the chance to become the kind of man that this country takes.

"But if he is the way he is, I'm the way I am too, and that night when I saw the terror on his face when he ran into the kitchen, I knew right then that I would never marry him."

When she stopped speaking Ben knew

that it was his cue to speak, to tell her what was on his mind, but he did not know how to say it. He was afraid that if he once opened up to her, he would not be able to stop and would pour out more of his heart than she would want to hear.

"Now that it's all over and you've gotten your man," Clarice prompted him, "what are you planning to do?"

"I don't know," Ben said. "Mr. Paulson said I could stay on as long as I want, an' in a way I want to stay . . . but in a way I want to go, too. The war, an' now all this killin' here, just has me confused. When I was a boy we had such a peaceful little world. There was never any questions I had to answer. It was just settled that when I got to be a man, I'd get me a piece of land somewhere near ma an' pa an' be a farmer like he was.

"That's what life was all about for us hill folks. His daddy was a farmer an' he was a farmer an' I was supposed to be a farmer who raised my young'uns to be farmers. Then the war come to us. It took longer to reach us because we were off, sort of isolated, an' none of us had slaves an' none of us wanted to fight for some other feller's politics. But it come an' it killed my pa an' took me away.

"Now I just don't know. My home's gone. I've killed more men than I can even remember. I've lived through hell an' eaten garbage an' acted like an animal for so long that I don't know who I am anymore."

Clarice's answer startled Ben. "Sounds like you've got a first-class case of feeling sorry for yourself," she said.

Ben looked up angrily at the girl and snapped, "I'm sorry. I thought you wanted to hear about how I felt, but I guess I was wrong."

"No, I do want to hear about it," she said, "but maybe it's time for you to change how you feel about yourself. You're not the first man who's come west with nothing but bad memories behind him. This country's filled with people who never had anything in their lives but hardship and suffering and disappointments, but the best of them have just learned to be more determined to make good lives for themselves because of it."

Ben wanted to be angry at her words, to get away from her and get on his horse and just leave for good, but part of him wanted to agree and to hear more about how men pulled the threads of their disappointing lives together and made something good for themselves.

"I just don't know how to go about figuring out the future," he said. "I've been living with different kinds of hates in me for so long that I guess now that all of them are over with, I don't know what to replace them with."

"Would it help if I said that I think I'm in love with you . . . ?" Clarice began hesitantly. Ben turned and studied her face. He only saw sincerity there.

". . . and that I think you love me, too," she continued.

For a moment Ben did not move, but finally he reached out his rough hand and touched her cheek lightly. "Who would have ever thought . . . ?" he said.

"I've thought it and known it for some time," Clarice said. "It's been in your eyes and in my heart when we've been alone together. I've known, but I thought that your silly male pride or some crazy idea that you weren't good enough for me was going to drive you away before —" She suddenly fell into his arms and, with her face buried against his shoulder, murmured, "I think I would have died if you had left me."

Stroking the back of her hair gently, he kept repeating to her, "I won't leave . . . I won't leave. . . ."

CHAPTER NINETEEN

Ben sat on the edge of the hotel room bed watching Ridge Parkman stuff the last of his few belongings into his saddlebags. He was trying to think of the appropriate words for what he felt, but everything that was coming out of his mouth seemed so trivial, so inadequate.

"If you ever get back this way, Ridge," he said, "I expect I'll be around here for a while."

Ridge looked up at him with a knowing grin and said, "I kinda figgered that, and believe me, I'm real glad for you."

"Things sorta worked out," Ben said.

"I might roam back this way one of these times. Once this war is wrapped up I'll be wantin' to work out West here, where the most things are goin' on. There's a lot of opportunities for a man out in this part of the country if he's got the stuff to get it. There's room enough for a man to sort of settle an' spread out, make a new start, an' nobody's goin' to worry too much about where he's been nor what he's done. It's young an' wild out here . . . an' it's free."

"It's a good place," Ben agreed, "with good folks."

When Ridge finished his packing he and Ben walked downstairs and outside where the stage was waiting. Ridge was going to ride it far enough to reach a railhead where he could catch a train back to Washington. A small group had gathered to see him off. To one side stood Paulson and his wife with the Morgan family, and on the other side was Sheriff Perkins and Paulson's crew of cowboys.

Ridge shook hands around with everybody before turning and walking to the stagecoach door. Ben was standing there waiting for him, and Clarice came over to stand by Ben's side. Looking at the two of them, Ridge said with a grin, "That's fine, real fine. If you had a sister, miss, I'd be tempted to linger in these parts myself."

"I guess they decided one was quite enough," Clarice said. She stepped up and gave Ridge a kiss on the cheek.

When Ridge turned to Ben they shook hands and Ben said, "Believe me, it'll be a long time before you'll be forgotten around here."

"Well, you've been a good pardner, too, Ben," Ridge said. "I'd trade just about any two men I've ever worked with for you, an' maybe throw in a little boot besides. But I don't guess there'd be much chance of persuadin' you to leave these parts."

"No chance," Clarice said.

Ridge got into the stage and closed the door without any further words. Ben, Clarice, and the others stood watching the stage until it disappeared from view at the edge of town.

The employees of Thorndike Press hope you have enjoyed this Large Print book. All our Thorndike, Wheeler, and Kennebec Large Print titles are designed for easy reading, and all our books are made to last. Other Thorndike Press Large Print books are available at your library, through selected bookstores, or directly from us.

For information about titles, please call:
(800) 223-1244

or visit our Web site at:
http://gale.cengage.com/thorndike

To share your comments, please write:
Publisher
Thorndike Press
10 Water St., Suite 310
Waterville, ME 04901